What Gathers at Dusk

AMBROSE IBSEN

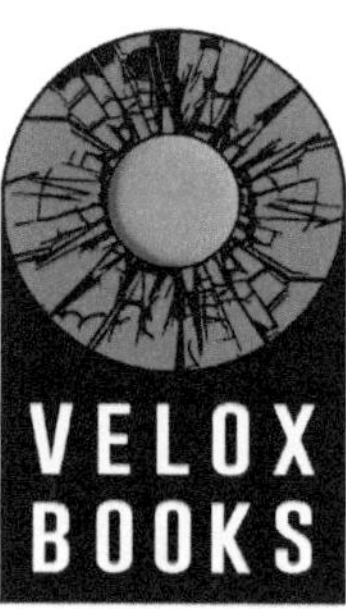

Published by arrangement with the author.

The story, all names, characters, and incidents portrayed in this production are fictitious. No identification with actual persons (living or deceased), places, buildings, and products is intended or should be inferred.

YOU'RE READING ANOTHER TERRIFYING COLLECTION FROM

**FOLLOW VELOX TO KEEP
THE NIGHTMARES COMING:**

Contents

Eating Alicia Morrison

THEY FOUND HER FACEDOWN in the earth. After a whole lot of pestering, the cops took me to the exact spot—right to the place where my girlfriend of eleven years, Alicia Morrison, was dumped by an unknown assailant.

It was a boggy area, overgrown with poison sumac, half-flooded from March to early September, and home to just about every insect you can think of. You can't drive over this stuff, meaning the guy who killed my beloved must've parked along the highway shoulder and carried her a mile-and-a-half before dumping her in the fen. Had some nerdy plant collector not passed through the area at just the right time, it's likely Alicia's body would never have been found.

She was in a poor state when the cops got there. Badly decomposed, half-digested by the local fauna. A matter-of-fact patrolman told me that when they first happened upon her body, it was so covered in flies and other wriggling pests they nearly missed her.

So, a few days after the funeral, I finally made it out there. I don't know why I insisted so much, why I just *had* to be there, but I felt the visit was gravely important. I needed closure and could think of no other place to get it. Of course, standing there in the bog after the cops took off, staring into a buggy puddle by myself, I found nothing of the sort. The heat was unbearable as I walked around and around the shallow pit. No matter how long I lingered there, I could make no sense of the insensible, could find no balm for my spirit. I had a lot of mourning left to do, but it fast became clear that this wasn't an ideal spot to meditate on my loss.

Human beings are superstitious and sentimental creatures. I wanted—*needed*—something to remember her by, however small. Alicia and I had been thinking of marrying when death stole her away, and I still wasn't sure how I'd carry on without her. A reminder of her, an emotional crutch, was a desperate necessity. For that reason, I took an empty soda bottle out of the car and filled it with bog water—water from the very spot where she'd been found. Under the circumstances, taking a little part of the site with me seemed the best I could do, even if it was strange.

With my memento in tow, I walked back to my car and drove off, utterly grief-stricken. That should have been the end of it; I should have spent days and weeks mourning Alicia and tending to my broken heart. In the hours after I returned home, that's exactly what my evening looked like.

But that night, as I tossed and turned in a delirium of anger and sadness, something happened that forever altered the course of the whole affair. Prior to bed, I had sat up looking at the bottle of bog water under the light of my nightstand lamp. The detritus-rich stuff had brimmed with life; aquatic insects and other critters were many, and my study of them had proven a pleasant, if momentary, distraction.

Sometime before dawn, however, I made the critical error of confusing said bottle of bog water for my bottle of nightly drinking water, and without realizing it, drank down half the infested liquid in a parched gulp.

My reaction was one of violent illness, of course. I put on my light and began retching. I clawed dried stems and bits of gravel from my tongue and tried to put the image of swamp critters swimming around in my gut out of my head. When the threat of nausea passed, however, and my shock had equalized back into the dreariness that was then my standard, I had a big laugh.

And more than that, in a fit of seeming madness, I guzzled down the remainder.

Perhaps, in my agitated state, I thought it perfectly fine to drink the water. It was foul stuff, yes—tasted miserable and likely brought with it myriad pathogens. On the other hand, my beloved's corpse had partially dissolved in that same water. The things living in it had feasted upon her. By partaking in it myself, I had unwittingly attained a posthumous closeness with Alicia that I had never expected.

This realization—that I now had traces of her in me, no matter how slight—was enough to soothe my sour mood, and I passed off to sleep not twenty minutes after draining the bottle.

A most curious thing happened in the hours before dawn.

I was plagued by dreams.

Not my own, however.

The visions that came to me were those of another mind, another time.

When I awoke, I felt reasonably sure that I'd hallucinated everything, but I can say now with certainty that there was no mistake. My initial instinct was correct.

Having consumed the bog water—and every iota of Alicia persisting within it—I was treated to a parade of her memories.

I saw Alicia's tenth birthday party—saw the gifts and cake that her mother brought out amid the mess of banners. I was serenaded by the party-goers, experiencing every sensation as only Alicia herself could have experienced it. I had the impression that I myself had lived this, had been present for it, though I knew I hadn't been. Alicia had been nineteen when we'd first met.

I had a vision of an argument she'd had with a high school friend, and another of a class trip to the art museum in middle school. I took in the Titians and the Caravaggios just as she'd done, as though the two of us shared one mind, one pair of eyes.

There is no rational explanation for what occurred that night. By ingesting trace amounts of Alicia, I had somehow ingested her essence, her memories.

Frankly, I had no interest in trying to explain it.

All I knew was that I had to acquire more of it.

Alicia was gone, but in this we still shared a connection.

Assessing the dissolved solids in a body of water is the work of scientists. Even for them, determining precisely what ratios of said solids are attributable to a corpse is probably impossible. Alicia's body had stewed in the bog for some weeks, bobbing in the drink like a noxious batch of sun tea, gradually sharing herself with the water and all its inhabitants.

I drove back to the spot the next morning, finding conditions cooler and more pleasant. Hiking to the spot where the officers had previously led me, I knelt beside the muddy pool and cupped another dose of the water into my mouth. There were dead flies in it, bits of other insects and traces of plant life, but I swallowed it all the same. You may ask yourself how I managed to do so without vomiting, and I can only say that I forced it all down in the interest of sooner reconnecting with my beloved. These flies and insects had likely fed on her corpse; thus, ingesting them in the brew despite my reservations was as natural as taking vitamins.

With a belly full of sloshing water, I returned to my car and rolled down the windows, opting to take a short rest behind the wheel. It wasn't long before the pleasant breeze lulled me and the quietness of the stretch allowed sleep to return in force.

And this time, again, it brought with it visions.

They were sharper than before. Clearer and more detailed.

They were not all pleasant to me, however.

There were old memories of sledding in the winter, followed by hot cocoa.

I had a vision of the two of us on an early date, where we'd dined at an Italian restaurant and gone to the movies afterward. I relished the sensation of us holding hands, delighted in our laughter and smiles.

There was one vision, though—a vision of Alicia with another man.

Handsome, clean-cut. My age, though certainly not me. What started with a few guarded kisses ultimately ended in the bedroom of her apartment. I recognized the fixtures, recognized the framed photo of Alicia and I on the nightstand. I did *not* recognize the man on top of her, however.

Judging by the depth of that memory, it appears that my lover enjoyed the encounter. I was spared no detail, and when I awoke in the driver's seat, I was in a cold sweat, sick to my stomach—and not solely on account of the filthy water I'd swilled.

Miserable and lonely, I had committed to this bizarre course in the hopes of reconnecting with my beloved Alicia.

Instead, I'd inadvertently discovered an infidelity.

She'd been cheating on me with this mystery man. I couldn't guess how long it'd been going on, or whether she'd been planning to leave me for him before her untimely end. I also wasn't sure who he was. A co-worker of hers I'd never met? Some random match on a dating app? I'd never seen him before—that was just about the only thing I *was* sure of.

I went shambling out of the car, hurt and confused.

Who was this man? Had he had a hand in Alicia's death? How long had she strung me along, playing faithful and innocent?

Returning to the bog, I was determined to get my answer.

It took me the better part of two days to empty the slimy divot in the ground and to process its writhing contents. The next two nights were packed with dream-visions of the kind I've already described—most of them innocent and heartwarming. Alicia's family get-togethers, meetings at work, road trips with friends, concerts, and plays...

I was presented, too, with more mental footage of the mystery man.

His fling with Alicia, it turned out, had not been brief. For a few seasons, at least—if one accounts for the weather from one vision to the next—they'd carried on behind my back in passionate abandon. Most of the encounters took place at Alicia's, likely on weekends when she'd claimed to be traveling for business. Fool that I'd been, I'd believed her—had never thought to check up.

Curiously, however, there were a couple of occasions when the trysts took place at the man's house.

And having drunk liter after liter of corpse-rich water, I was presented with such neat and tidy visions of their meetings that I could begin to make out certain important details.

I experienced a vision of Alicia driving down Waterman Street in the late autumn. I watched her pull her car into a driveway—the driveway of a house whose mailbox wore the numerals 4-1-4, with a mess of scraggly shrubs out front and a tall pine tree near its sidewalk.

Living through Alicia's visions, I now knew where I could find the man.

I didn't know his name, but I had his address firmly in mind. I weighed the possibility of paying him a visit, of revealing that I knew of their hookups. I considered investigating whether he'd had anything to do with Alicia's death.

I ultimately decided to hop in my car and follow the same route Alicia had shown me in my dreams. I wanted to speak to the man, to give him a piece of my mind, at least.

But before doing so, I stopped and bought a gun.

The house looks exactly the way it did in my dreams. The driveway's been repaved since their last booty call, and the pine is in need of a good trim, but the moment it enters into view a shiver runs down my spine and I feel like I've been there before.

A deep breath. Kill the engine. I plant a firm knock on the door; then, after a few seconds, another.

The man himself answers the summons. Handsome, yes. A little haggard. Has he been mourning, too? I can't tell at a glance. "Can I help you?" he asks, looking me over curiously.

Now that I'm here, I don't know what to do, what to say. I open my mouth and just blurt, "I know about you and Alicia."

His eyes go wide for a second. He seems taken aback. Then, probably putting two-and-two together, he shows some signs of shame. "Oh... Oh, man. You're the boyfriend, I take it?"

I nod.

He sighs, runs his hand through his hair. Sports an uncomfortable smile. "Listen, man, I'm sorry."

"Yeah?"

"Look, when I first met her, I didn't know she was seeing anyone."

"Right."

"It was never my intention to step on your toes. Had I known, I wouldn't have gotten involved."

"Right, right."

"She was a wonderful girl."

"She was."

"After everything that's happened…" He shakes his head. "It's a lot. Messed-up world out there."

"Yeah, it is." I point back to my car. "Listen, can I show you something?"

"Huh?"

Again, I motion to the car. "Will you… come with me for a bit? There's something I want to show you. Something I think you ought to see."

His smile gets more uncomfortable. He isn't the least bit interested. "Uh… no, thanks, man. Listen, I'm sorry about everything, but—"

It's wrong of me to act like I'm giving him a choice. I pull the handgun out of my waistband and press it against his stomach. The muzzle is resting on his impressive abs, just like Alicia's head used to do after bouts of lovemaking. "Car. Now."

He isn't dumb enough to resist. He puts his hands up and tries to defuse the situation. "W-Whoa, dude, come on, we can talk this out. Please, put that away."

Before he knows it, he's making these same appeals from my passenger seat as I'm speeding down the road. I hit eighty before I even make it to the highway. I keep one eye on him, my finger on the trigger and gun pointed at his center of mass, while screaming down the fast lane. He's blathering, white in the face, and all I'll tell him is, "Bud, there's something I've gotta show you."

Now we're there, on the side of the highway, in the middle of nowhere. He's marching out in front of me, the gun pressed to the small of his back. He's got his head low like a prisoner of war, expecting the worst.

Finally, we make it to the spot. "Look here," I say. "This is it."

"This is *what?*"

"This is where her body was dumped," I explain. "She was thrown into this ditch. It was full of water. Her body broke down. Cops almost didn't find it."

"Shit…"

"I know you were screwing her," I continue. "But... did you have anything to do with *this?*"

"What?" he asks. "Y-You're asking me if I murdered her?"

"That's right."

"No! No, of course not!"

"You sure about that? You lying to me?"

"No! I-I cared for her, all right? I wouldn't... I would never..."

"You cared about her? Interesting."

"I mean it! I'm telling the truth here, man!"

"All right," I reply. "Turn around. Nice and slow."

"Y-You believe me, right?" He turns around, tears in his eyes, hands held high.

By way of answer, I slot two rounds neatly into his forehead and watch his limp body topple into the soggy crevasse.

Then, sitting down on the muddy ground, I wait.

It's going to take a while. The scenery is going to have to feed before I can get the answers I'm looking for. We're going to need a bit of rain, too, before the process begins and I can get his side of the story. There's plenty of time, though; the genius of this particular spot is that a body was only recently fished out of it. No one's going to expect a new corpse here, not now.

When I can finally drink him in, then and only then will I know if he was telling the truth.

This way, he won't be able to lie to me. I'll see it all through his very eyes.

Something I've learned far too late in life is that you can't always take people at their word. Sometimes, you have to go the extra mile to keep 'em honest.

Alicia taught me that.

Home Again, Home Again

Eight-and-a-half years. That's how long it'd been since I—or *anyone*—had last seen my older sister, Sabrina.

She ran away from home at seventeen, just before graduating high school. On account of her age, the cops got involved right away. Every lead dried up, though, and after a few months her face was replaced by others on the posters at the local stores. We made fliers of our own, appealed to the local and statewide news, but nothing much ever came of all that.

Drugged-up hitchhikers matching Sabrina's description were spotted as far away as Duluth, but tended to vanish before the cops could locate them. A while after my sister's face was broadcast on a major network, the remains of a body were found in a flooded drainage ditch seventy-odd miles from our hometown, and my mother was called to the site. Unfortunately, the elements had broken down the evidence so completely that the resulting goo proved useless to forensics. No positive ID could be made. Again, we were denied closure.

The men on the case, very sorrowful in their way but run off their feet, assured us that the corpse in the bog was *probably* Sabrina—a conclusion that my mother simply refused to accept.

And so, even when the case went ice cold, my poor mom kept waiting up, night after night, for her daughter to return. She was certain that Sabrina was still out there somewhere, and I soon tired of attempting to convince her otherwise. I and everyone else in our town knew that Sabrina was never coming home.

That's why, when the text message came in at a quarter to midnight, I could hardly believe my eyes.

Sam, your sister's home! After all these years, she's really back! my mother wrote. *Please, come home as soon as you get this message!*

The weight of eight-and-a-half years hit me like a tidal wave, and after rereading the message several times I went running out of my apartment and jumped in the car. I didn't know what to think; I was out of my head with excitement and gratitude, though there were other things in the mix, too, which plagued me as I booked it through the empty streets. Incredulity, hints of bitterness for such a long absence—these and other emotions weighed down the sharp air. I ran red lights, breezed through four-way stops, fallen leaves rustling raucously in my wake.

Sabrina had been gone almost a decade, and everyone except my mother had written her off as dead.

Now, unbelievably, she was back.

I expected a flurry of flashing lights, at least a few police cars on the lawn and neighbors rubbernecking from across the street, but as I pulled into the old neighborhood and approached the house, I found none of that. The porch light was still burning, but that was all.

I eased my car into the driveway and killed the engine. I didn't even bother locking up; I rushed out and went straight for the screen door, ripping it open and almost tripping over the threshold. "Ma?" I called into the warm house. "Ma?"

The TV was murmuring in its usual corner, and a tepid cup of half-finished tea sat on the collapsible tray beside the rumpled sofa. The light in the kitchen was on, but as I charged across the living room I found the kitchen and dinette unoccupied. "Ma?"

"Sam?" A faint voice reached my ears from somewhere down the hall to my left, and as I turned in search of its source I discovered a light coming from the rear bedroom—Sabrina's old room.

It'd been many years since I'd last heard that voice. "S-Sabrina?" Immediately I hurried down the hall and hooked a right into the dimly-lit doorway, and there, on the bed my mother had dutifully laundered and remade for over eight years, I found a slender woman seated, hands bunched in her lap, brown hair hanging low in oily ringlets and green eyes cast even lower.

My sister stirred a little as I walked in, and she turned her pale face to meet mine, fixing it into an odd expression. She didn't look happy, but she didn't strike me as entirely sad; the look transmitted something more subtle, a mood that lived somewhere in the vast gulf between the two. Nervousness. Shame, maybe. The smile that spread across her lips was a shaky and inconstant thing. "Hello, Sam," she said in a voice barely higher than a whisper. "It's... It's been a long time, hasn't it?"

I didn't know what to say. Certainly, it *had* been a long time—a long *and painful* time. I was facing someone I had never expected to see again, had been given an opportunity I had never expected to receive. Many words approached my tongue as I stood there in the doorway, stupefied. Some were kind, others were barbed. What I most wanted to say was: "*You'd better have a good excuse for the past eight years...*" The words I spoke instead were these: "I thought... I thought you were dead."

Sabrina had her back to the open window, so that the moonlight clung to her delicate frame and set it off against the gloom of the room's interior. The old lamp to the left of her, on the nightstand, was burning beneath the dusty shade she'd once decorated with quotations in Sharpie. To the right was her dresser, along with the tall mirror whose corners were crowded with curling Polaroids of friends and pictures of pop stars she'd carved out of magazines.

In a word, Sabrina looked filthy. Her baggy white sweatshirt had been stained gray-black by too many tours of service, and the frayed ends of her jean shorts gave way to grimy knees and filth-streaked legs. She was wearing a cheap pair of flip-flops that looked ready to give out with the next step, and her toenails were studded with murk as though it were chipped nail polish. Her fingernails were similarly jagged and dirty.

She looked as though she'd been living on the streets for some time. That was how it seemed to me as I studied her from across the room. She sniffed and ran her palms over her face, forcing another smile past shaky lips. "So... I'm sure you have a lot of questions..." she said, clearing her throat. "I, uh... I know you and mom are both going to have a lot of questions. And... you deserve answers, of course..."

I nodded slowly. "Yeah, well..." Turning back into the hall, I paused. "Where *is* mom, anyhow? She texted me, asked me to come by, but she wasn't out in the living room when I came in." The other rooms along the hall were dark, bathroom included.

"I'm not sure," replied my sister. "She was in here just a few minutes ago..."

Now that we were on the subject, I found myself bothered by my mother's absence. Here, her beloved daughter, eight years gone, had returned, and where was *she?* I couldn't imagine anything taking precedence over this reunion, especially at so late an hour. What was she up to?

Sabrina leaned forward, ready to launch into her lengthy explanations, but I cut her short. "Hold on," I said. "Let me grab mom real quick."

"Sam, wait—"

"No," I interjected. "You said it yourself. She and I both deserve answers. She's going to want to hear this."

Defeatedly, Sabrina nodded and eased back down onto the edge of the bed.

Slipping down the hall, I returned to the living room and stood at the threshold to the kitchen. "Ma? Ma, where'd you go?" I called out.

There was no reply.

I paced across the kitchen and then opened the side door leading into the garage. Her sedan was still there. The cold concrete floors were cluttered with boxes, gardening supplies, and more, but I found no sign of her as I looked in from the kitchen doorway. Next, I moved to the backyard, passing through the stubborn screen door that whined on its unoiled hinges. There, the empty flowerbeds were hidden under carpets of dead leaves, the bird feeder swayed in the icy breeze, and various creatures lent their voices to a low nocturnal chorus. But once again, there was no sign of my mother.

I was at my wit's end when I locked the back door and trudged into the kitchen, warming my hands in my pockets. Pulling out my phone, I decided to send her a text. It was just barely possible that she'd stepped out—that she'd contacted law enforcement and was giving officers the necessary details to close Sabrina's case for good. I tapped out a quick message: *Ma, I'm home. Where are you?*

From somewhere close at hand, a sudden chirp shattered the silence.

It wasn't the call of a night bird. It wasn't the musing of a cricket. It was an artificial noise; sharp, bordering on irritating. A noise I knew well.

I recognized it at once as my mother's text tone—sounding, no doubt, on account of the message I'd fired off just seconds before. She was close by, apparently. Or, at least, her phone was. "*Ma?*" I froze in place, ears groping the air for every last hint of the high-pitched tone.

It seemed to be coming from across the kitchen—specifically, from the small laundry room beside the dinette. This was the one place in the house I hadn't thought to check, and I now saw that the slim door leading to it sat ajar. A thick darkness lived on the other side of the white jamb, and as I stood by the sink, bewildered, that same darkness was momentarily pierced by a bright glow.

The glow, perhaps, of a cell phone spitting out notifications.

"Ma?" My voice was quiet as I walked around the dinner table and approached the door. I eased it open carefully and stepped inside just as the white glow cut out, leaving me stranded in the darkness. Though I pushed at the door, the kitchen chairs on the other side kept me from opening it fully, and the washer and dryer, not to mention the laundry baskets and boxes stacked on either side of me, blocked out much of the outer light. I swept the inside of the doorway with my palm, but upon hitting the light switch discovered that the bulb overhead was either dead or missing.

I reached, then, for my phone, preparing to turn on the flashlight. Before I could do so, however, the white glow returned, rupturing the blackness for one horrible instant.

And in that instant, I realized I was not alone in the laundry room.

A cell phone gripped in rigid hands lit up in answer to my earlier text. A pale, staring face, with eyes of glass, was revealed by the screen's glow—my mother's. She was seated on the floor, half-curled with her back against the wall, her lips knotted in a dreadful scowl and her gaze as wide as it was vacant.

"M-Ma!" I rushed to her, dropped to my knees and tended to her, though before the glow of her phone died out and I lost my view of her dreadful, frozen face I knew she was dead. There was no blood at the scene, no clear wounds or signs of struggle. Had it been a heart attack? A stroke? The way I found her, tucked against the wall in a fearful posture, suggested she'd been confronted with something traumatizing or terrifying in the end.

I took my mother's phone and crawled out of the laundry room half-hysterical. Bumping against kitchen chairs and knocking the table out of place, I sucked in a few deep breaths and shambled over to the sink, where my stomach threatened a mutiny. What was I to do? How could I break this news to Sabrina, who'd only just returned home?

When I'd gotten ahold of myself, I took my mother's phone into the backyard and prepared to call 9-1-1. My shaky thumb went searching for the phone icon, but I soon realized that the messaging app was still up and running—and before I could close it, something caught my eye. I discovered something unexpected in the text window. My mother had drafted a long, rambling message at some point, but had failed to send it.

DON'T COME HOME, SAM. DON'T COME HOME. IT'S NOT YOUR SISTER. IT ISN'T SABRINA. I DON'T KNOW WHAT IT IS, BUT IT'S NOT YOUR SISTER. IT LOOKS LIKE HER. IT TALKS LIKE HER. IT'S IN THE HOUSE, BUT IT'S NOT HER. DON'T COME HERE, SAM. DON'T COME INSIDE. I CAN HEAR HER FROM THE OTHER ROOM. SHE'S COMING. SHE'S COMING—

My mother had written that all out in evident panic while hiding in the laundry room, and death had taken her before she'd been able to hit SEND. Baffled, I read the message again, pacing across the yard. What was this supposed to mean? Had my mother suffered from hallucinations before dying? A psychotic break? I'd spoken to Sabrina just minutes ago; the unsent message was clearly the work of a deluded mind.

My panicked pacing through the yard brought me just a stone's throw from my sister's open window. Glancing into her room, I found her still seated upon the bed with her back to me, oblivious to the horrible discovery I'd made in the laundry room. I felt sick with grief, my nerves pulled so tight they were on the verge of snapping like guitar strings. *How am I going to break this news to her?* I wondered. *After all we've been through... and after Sabrina finally came home... we have to suffer THIS?*

Dizzy and bleary-eyed, I stood there, wondering what to say to the emergency dispatcher.

And then, unexpectedly, a shiver shot down my spine.

It wasn't the cool autumn air that did it. It wasn't even the memory of my poor mother's huddled corpse in the laundry room that made me shudder.

I shivered because there were eyes on me.

I could feel myself being studied, probed by an alien gaze. Buried in suburban silence with only the rustling of leaves for company, I scanned the thinning bushes and trees, surveyed nearby yards and windows, seeing no one.

No one, that is, except for Sabrina, still seated on the bed, just a few yards away.

She had her back to me, head low. I knew that she wasn't looking at me, and yet the longer I peered in through the window, the surer I was that the unwelcome attention was pouring from her. I took a few quiet steps toward the house, bringing the inside of Sabrina's room into sharper focus.

I spied the wrinkled bedspread, the borders of a dusty shelf crowded with books and old plushies, the hazy outline of the bedroom doorway opposite the window, and the edge of the lamp on her nightstand.

And then I happened to glance at the mirror.

The streaky mirror sat atop the dresser, to Sabrina's right, and from where I stood there was light enough to study the scene reflected in it. Everything captured in the mirror was precisely as I've just described it—save one very important thing.

My sister was seated on the bed, right where I'd left her, but the Sabrina I knew was *not* visible in the mirror. Something else was reflected there, where she should have been.

The figure in the reflection was gaunt and bare, with skin as splotchy and dark as black mold. It maintained the same posture my sister did; shoulders stooped, head low, hands perched upon the mattress as if for support. Unlike the Sabrina I'd left behind in the room, however, the reflected figure's eyes were not rooted to the floor. Instead, by a subtle turn of the head, it had focused its oozing greenish gaze upon the mirror.

Through this act of discreet surveillance, it revealed a grinning and skull-like countenance whose only covering was a thin and clinging film of blackish, rubbery flesh. Damp orbs the color of moss answered for eyes in the thing's wide sockets, and these were fixed on me with such demonic interest that I would not have been surprised had they slithered free and come to the window themselves.

I was not merely being watched. I was being anticipated. The distraught figure on the bed was an illusion, mere bait, meant to draw me in. Something had come to this house, wrapped snugly in illusions, but in the moonlit mirror its cover had slipped. My mother had seen through it—though far too late.

As I stood shuddering in the yard, I had the impression that the figure was not fully aware of my understanding; that it didn't realize I'd seen through the ruse. It grinned and watched with the perverse satisfaction of a predator in hiding, savoring the deception. Its pride, its delight—these alone were enough to strike me nauseous with fear.

I did everything I could to telegraph calm and ignorance of the truth. Backing away, the mirror fell from sight. I stood against the side of the house, moving away from the window.

From inside the room, I heard a faint stirring upon the bed. "Sam? Is everything all right, Sam?" came my sister's voice. "Please, come back in. We have so much to talk about..."

I didn't bother replying until I was sure I could do so without stammering. "Everything's fine, Sabrina. I was just looking for mom."

There was a brief silence—a silence in which I could *feel* the fiend's smile widening even as I cowered against the siding. "I see. And did you *find* her?" asked the thing on my sister's bed in a mocking, honeyed tone.

"No…" I lied. "No, I didn't." I squeezed my mother's phone. "I'll be back inside in just a minute."

The figure said nothing.

Taking a deep breath, I started slowly past the window, as if heading back into the house. I trudged through the yard with all the nonchalance I could feign, but there was no subduing my fright when I passed the open window and caught sight of my sister's room in my periphery.

She was sitting on the other side of the bed now, staring out the window.

Sabrina—filthy, bedraggled, yet smiling sedately—followed me with her green eyes. She sat just a few feet from the screen, hands in her lap and head cocked to the side so that her tangled hair spilled messily across her face.

Walking slowly, steadily, just then, was one of the hardest things I've ever done. Instinct told me to run—to *sprint*—for my life. Only by a herculean effort was I able to calmly reach the edge of the backyard fence. Hitching a leg over carefully, I tried not to rattle the chain-links and then hoisted myself over. Then, stealing past the garage, I found the driveway.

I was in my car with the engine running within seconds, and I pulled out as fast as I could without so much as glancing in the rearview.

It was in the bright lot of a 24-hour pharmacy, several miles away, that I finally fired up my mother's phone and called the cops.

What happened next, though, still haunts me.

The night grew darker, the autumn wind colder. A mass of police cruisers arrived outside my mother's house, and after I told the responding officers everything, the premises were stormed. I explained that there'd been an intruder, someone pretending to be my long-lost sister—though I didn't elaborate much on the strange and frightening nature of this figure. I admitted, too, that I'd found my mother in the laundry room, unresponsive. I stood in the street with a pair of officers while the rest entered the house, looking on with bated breath.

When all was said and done, I wasn't surprised that there were no signs of the figure in the back room. The counterfeit Sabrina was nowhere to be found. "She probably bailed before we got here," one officer theorized.

I *was* surprised, however, when the officers began filing out of the house and claimed, after a search of more than an hour, that my mother's body was also missing. The laundry room had been thoroughly checked, but they'd found no evidence of a body or any struggle within.

I have been assured that both are being sought by the authorities—that the local PD is doing everything in its power to track them both down.

If I'm honest, I hope they're never found.

I lay awake some nights, especially those cold and cloudy ones in mid-autumn, and wonder if my sister or mother will one day arrive at my doorstep, asking to be let in. In the future, things garbed in their essence may rap at my door in the dead of night, plaintively seeking admittance. *"It's been a long time. We have so much to discuss..."* they'll say. *"Please, let me in, Sam."*

Should that day come, I intend to keep my door locked.

For years after Sabrina's disappearance, my mother hoped for her return. She maintained a place for Sabrina in her home, spoke of her constantly as if she was on the verge of coming back, and kept the porch light on perpetually, as a beacon. In a sense, I believe that my mother's years of yearning and desperation drew that opportunistic thing to her door.

I've mourned my mother and sister, but unlike my mother, I've made peace with loss. I won't spend the rest of my life pining for a reunion, but will try to hold onto the good memories. The alternative—wishing and waiting for something I can't have—is far more dangerous. Wishes cast carelessly into the void sometimes come true; desperate whispers of the heart do not always go unheard. If you leave your porch light on long enough, something is sure to come shambling out of the gloom eventually...

It Waits Along the Left-Hand Path

Do you remember what it was like, being a kid? Were you wild and free, or cloistered?

My childhood fell into the first category. There were days when I'd step out the front door after breakfast, and I wouldn't come home until the cars on the lonesome country roads were putting on their headlights. Out there, in the fields and woods, I got stung by just about every critter that's got a stinger. Popping wheelies on my bike, I busted up my knees more times than I can count. You can still see the scars. I almost drowned while fishing for bluegill in the creek after a few days of heavy rain—*twice*.

I can look back at the bumps and the bruises, the scares, and laugh about it all now. Compared to a lot of kids today, sheltered and screen-addicted, my childhood looks like something out of the movies. A lot of little ones today have never *seen* a firefly, much less caught a jarful on a summer's night as I used to do. I like to think that the adventures of my childhood built a lot of character—that they made me more resilient. More imaginative, maybe.

But, of course, there are times when I look back on it all and wish my folks had been a little more restrictive. The older I get, the more I wish someone had kept a closer eye on me—denied me some of that freedom. Had they done so, I wouldn't have been there that summer evening, by the old bunker.

I wouldn't have been there the day that Jonah went missing.

Picture, if you will, a vast, *vast* sea of knee-high grass. Now throw a few clusters of woods into the mix, here and there, wherever you like. Oaks, jack pines, box elders—we had 'em all. Still with me? Imagine a few streams, ponds, and lakes spread out across this scenery, and long, winding roads throughout it that don't see a whole lot of traffic. You now have, in your mind, a pretty accurate illustration of the place I grew up.

Sure, there were some other bits and bobs. A steel mill, where fully half the town's men worked—and some of the women, too. A single school building answered for grades K through 12 and looked like a prison, with a tall wire fence around its perimeter. We had the quaintest big-box store you've ever seen in your life and a few restaurants that catered mainly to truckers. The houses all looked tired, even back then—not broken-down, not particularly dirty or messy, but like they'd had the wind knocked out of them. They tend to sit on generous lots; you might have to walk a few minutes to visit your nearest neighbor.

For kids, bikes were a must. There was just too much ground to cover. We'd pedal back and forth to school in flocks, taking the things along the shoulders of country roads while begging guys in big rigs to blast their horns. Most of us didn't have *nice* bikes. I myself piloted whatever cast-offs I could find at garage sales and kept them in working order with elbow grease.

Jonah, though, had a *really* nice bike. The day his dad brought it home from the shop—a silver Schwinn—he went blasting around town and drew the eye of every kid for miles. He was a quiet one, a little tall for his age, with sandy brown hair and oversized ears. His mother had passed on shortly after giving birth to him, and he lived with his dad, a manager at the steel mill, on my street, just three houses down.

Growing up in the days before video games and the internet, we had to make our own fun, and for a bunch of bored kids, that usually involved fist-fighting or unnecessary drama. Unlike most of us, Jonah was never one for those sorts of things. Cool-headed, he didn't get involved in the neighborhood spats and was well-liked by pretty much everyone. He was always willing to join the rest of us in exploring town, looking for something interesting to do, but at the first whiff of trouble, he had no qualms about striking out on his own and entertaining himself.

I think that's how he happened to find the bunker one day.

It doesn't matter how hard I look, what terms I use to search: I can't find anything official about the abandoned underground bunker. Believe me, I've tried just about everything I can think of, but even the older folks in town simply shrug their shoulders when the topic gets brought up. It's as though the structure has always been out there, waiting in the overgrown earth, its entrance shadowed by old-growth trees...

The best guess I or anyone else can come up with is that it was built during the Second World War. Some paranoiac with money, maybe, used to own the acreage in question and spent a pretty penny building a labyrinthine bunker underground to protect himself from potential air raids. Some have theorized, and I don't fully discount the notion, that the bunkers are a throwback to the Cold War era—built by the government in case of Russian nukes. A more benign idea that sometimes gets thrown around is that it isn't an underground bunker at all but a foundation for a long-abandoned factory or other commercial venture that never got off the ground. Seems plausible enough.

Whatever it is, none of us kids were really aware of its existence until the day that Jonah rode out on his own and went wandering through the woods north of town. To hear him tell it, he'd been on the lookout for frogs when he'd discovered what looked like a large metal pipe sticking out of the forest floor. Curved like the top of a candy cane and thoroughly rusted, he'd kicked at the thing and tried looking into it, finding only darkness and the scent of damp. As one does, he'd gone on to throw a bunch of pebbles and sticks into it in an effort to gauge the pipe's depth and had found it to run quite deep.

The next afternoon, after school, Jonah rounded all of us up and announced his find. "Yesterday, in the woods up north, I found something real weird. There are pipes sticking up out of the ground, and I think they lead to something."

I remember one of the other boys commenting, "Might be a gas pipe. Careful around those—you might blow something up."

"No," insisted Jonah, "This wasn't no gas pipe. I dropped something in, and I could hear it hit solid ground after a bit. I think... I think there's something underground, beneath the pipes. A room, maybe..."

Needless to say, this assertion caused quite a stir among us, and we didn't need any further convincing to explore that patch of woods. Arguing amongst ourselves—some taking Jonah's side and others sure that he was making it all up—we flew on our bikes and traced the route he'd taken the previous afternoon. Abandoning our rides on the grassy shoulder by the road, we went stomping into the woods.

It wasn't long before we discovered the first curved pipe. It was thick, growing out of the earth like some kind of rusted pitcher plant, its flared edges flaking away and its mouth filled with darkness. Like Jonah had done, we all took turns feeding stones and other junk into the pipe, attempting to sound its depths.

Wandering a little deeper in, one of the kids discovered another pipe—same size, shape, and condition as the other one. A third turned up shortly thereafter. I think we found five in total before we wandered far enough into the woods to happen upon something far more interesting.

Nestled in a little ridge, sheltered by shaggy trees and mounds of overgrowth, we found what looked to be a concrete doorway or tunnel set into the earth. When we first set eyes on it, I remember we all stopped dead in utter awe. It was like standing before the sealed door of Tutankhamen's tomb. The thick panels of the doorway were half-covered in moss and had obviously been set into the hillside long ago. The opening itself was covered by a large, warped panel—a thick piece of wood that answered for a door.

Us kids, we were intoxicated with excitement just then, believing that we'd found the home of some mystical, hill-dwelling being. Looking back now, though, a shiver runs down my spine when I think about that covered entryway. It never occurred to us to ask who had placed that great board there, or why the entrance had been blocked, or whether this mysterious site was private property. Why, it didn't even occur to us that someone or something dangerous might lurk inside; all we saw was the potential for adventure.

Despite the thrill of discovery, we knew in our guts that we'd stumbled upon something truly singular, and we did a good job, most of us, of not getting carried away. That's why, even after we carefully pulled back the board and stared into the night-dark entrance of the bunker, none of us actually went in.

None of us except for Jonah, that is.

I can still remember the way he stepped into the doorway, squinting into the murk and running his hands against the mossy walls of the interior. "Who *knows* what could be in here!" he said, glancing at each of us in turn. From the entryway, without a flashlight, there was really no telling what awaited us inside. Jonah seemed to sense our reticence and took it upon himself to act as the canary to our coal mine operation. "I'm going in," he told us. "I'll let you know what I find."

We didn't dissuade him. We didn't warn him of the risks, didn't even think to postpone his entry until we could get our hands on a flashlight. We all just stood around the mouth of this bunker and watched him slowly pace into the shadows; curious cowards, the lot of us. It was all concrete. The floors were a little textured, and I could tell that the walls were painted a faint blue. Jonah's Converse drummed out a steady beat as he went in, and the longer we listened, the quieter and more distant those steps became.

After a few minutes, his footsteps died away entirely. The sound was eaten up by the inner earth, snuffed out. Some of us, I think, had almost found our nerve and were thinking about venturing in. I remember I called to Jonah feebly from the entrance, something like, "Hey, how's it going in there? Find anything cool?"

But there was no answer.

I was soon joined by a chorus. We began calling out his name, every repetition more fraught with panic than the last. We stretched out the vowels, "*Joooonaaaaah!*" but still couldn't hear a reply. The air tumbling out of the bunker was moist and scented with rot. The bravest among us would take a couple of steps into the complex only to suddenly back out, as though the thick darkness within amounted to something tangible and impenetrable.

Fifteen, twenty minutes on, there was no more excitement in us, only fear. We started to freak out. Our cries became infrequent, and plans were being drafted to either storm in and seek him out or to pedal back home at double-quick speed. Knowing what came next, I'm ashamed to admit I was in the latter camp.

We hadn't heard Jonah's step in some time when the silence was suddenly pierced by a scream from deep within the bunker. A nightmarish sound, it came in a single, seconds-long burst, so forceful and terror-soaked that it knocked a few of us onto our asses. If you can believe it, though, what came next was much, *much* scarier for all of us.

Silence. When the scream ended, when the cold walls of stone managed to shake off its jarring echo, nothing came to take its place.

Some kids in this situation, you know, they like to have a little fun. They'll scream or make a scene just to shock their friends. All of us knew immediately that Jonah's scream hadn't been a put-on, though. He'd never been the kind of kid to play such tricks; it simply wasn't his style. If a nice, cool-headed kid like him was screaming about something, then there was a damn good reason for it.

Whatever discussions we'd been engaged in up to that point, we shut our mouths upon hearing that scream and abandoned ship. It was every man for himself; we sprinted through the woods, sought out our bikes by the road, and pedaled like we were competing in the Tour de France. We didn't have cell phones back then, and wouldn't you know it, there weren't any motorists to flag down for help at that moment, either. We had to bike all the way home, almost in tears, before we found someone we could tell—and it was a few minutes after that before our parents were able to get the details out of us clearly enough to pass them on to the sheriff.

The authorities looked for him. Hell, *half the town* must have gone looking for him; volunteers, young and old, filled those woods off and on for the next week. It was a proper search and rescue. Regardless, they never found him—not a trace of the boy *ever* turned up. I'm told they brought dogs into the bunker, lights, cops from the next county over.

Nothing. They couldn't turn up one single sign of Jonah—save, of course, for the silver Schwinn still resting in the grass by the road, where he'd left it.

Rewards were set, and for a little while there the adults in town tried to act optimistic. By fall, though, they stopped saying his name altogether; the entire incident was swept under the rug and seldom spoken of. Only one thing changed: Every kid in town was forbidden, *absolutely forbidden*, by parents and cops both, from hanging around in those woods north of town. The bunker, whatever its initial allure, was strictly off-limits now.

I'm not a child anymore, though. The sheriff who made that decree has long since retired, and—after a few decades of studiously avoiding that patch of northern woods—most of the locals have seemingly forgotten the bunker altogether. *I* never did have the luxury of forgetting, though. I bump into my memories of the place now and then—in dreams and in waking life. It's like an itch you can't reach; when it turns up, you just have to ignore it until it goes away.

One day, recently, I decided to scratch that itch the only way I knew how.

I was in town, visiting my family for the first time in ages, when I sought out the bunker and explored it for myself. A few days before driving in, I'd dreamt of the incident, had been haunted by Jonah's scream across the gulf of years, and had gotten it into my head that, being a grown man, I could now do what I'd lacked the courage to do as a boy. I knew I wouldn't find anything in there that would give me closure about Jonah's fate. It'd been decades, far too long for evidence of that kind to still be kicking around. Still, I wagered that facing my fears and conquering that shadowed haunt of my youth could only be therapeutic.

So, hopping on the northbound after lunch with my folks, I came to a screeching halt outside that patch of woods—far denser than I remembered it—and parked my sedan in the grass the way I'd once dumped my bike.

Though trauma had pretty well imprinted the lay of the land upon my mind, I had a good deal more trouble tracking down the boarded entrance than one might expect. The available landmarks—that is, the curved pipes sticking out of the ground—had been worn almost to stubs by the additional decades of exposure, so I had nothing much to go by. I wandered half-aimlessly between the trees, investigating the clefts in every hill, the nooks in each shallow valley.

The bunker entrance rather snuck up on me. One moment, I was bumbling around in the warm woods, growing irritated and entertaining the possibility of throwing in the towel. The next, I happened to slip a little while navigating a wild ravine, and the doorway came into soft focus through the greenery. The way the foliage had parted in a light breeze to reveal the concrete doorway, the warped panel of timber still clinging to the opening, I felt almost as though it had winked at me. *Welcome back. It's been a while, hasn't it?*

Twenty years and more separated this encounter with the bunker from my first. How was it, then, that nothing had changed? I don't mean that in a poetic sense; as I stood there, peeling back the crooked board and staring into the yawning mouth of the underground complex, I was struck by the scene's perfect fidelity to my memory of it. It was as though the clinging weeds and swaying grasses, even the towering box elders overhead, had ceased growing the day Jonah had gone missing. The stony borders of the structure, jutting from the hill as they did, were no more cracked or pitted than they had been the first go-round, despite having weathered a good many more winters. I wondered, then scoffed at, the idea that I'd somehow stepped back in time by returning there. That seemed the simplest explanation for the bewildering lack of change, anyhow.

As kids, we'd come unprepared. Now, with a cell phone in my pocket, a flashlight in hand, and a pair of solid boots on, I fancied myself ready for just about anything and went shuffling in, my dull tread echoing against the moss-grown walls the way Jonah's had all those years ago. Though a good deal of the paint had begun to chip off, the walls retained a bluish hue. Early on, I found only solid concrete above me, though a little further in

I spied long successions of piping, much of it reduced to rusted ruin, that spanned the length of the initial corridor. That corridor, terminating in leftward and rightward bends that promised access to remoter strata, reeked of dust and earth and damp.

It occurred to me, then, as I weighed the two avenues available to me, that I didn't really know what I had gotten myself into. Like Jonah, I was on the cusp of plunging myself into a subterranean maze, and there were no guarantees that I would be able to find my way out again, even with a flashlight. I admit I waffled for a moment, walked a few paces down each of the available paths, before simply charging to the right.

The enormity of the bunker shocked me; it proved to have a tremendous footprint, and in no way had I expected the succession of passages and rooms that stemmed from this rightward branch. I found chamber after chamber, each of them empty except for the traces of nature that had stolen in. The stems of creeping vines had ingratiated themselves in rare cracks, bearing dark green leaves and rock-hard buds in the absence of sun. The further I ventured, the more I encountered flooding; many rooms and hallways were filled with standing water, and it was from these rust-colored pools that the complex's most notable smells emanated. I supposed that the structure, aged and given over to disrepair, was no longer watertight, and that heavy rains or changes in the water table had wreaked havoc.

Mind you, all this was glimpsed in heavy shadow—shadow burdensome enough to add real weight to the air and slow my step. Natural light had never touched these meandering tunnels, and the darkness that lived in them now clung bat-like to the walls and corners. It was true enough that men had built the bunker, yes—but in its current state, it had become the haunt of other things, with unique energies of their own. But *what?* There were simply no signs of life anywhere in evidence. I spied not a single insect or small animal in all my time there, and the lack was concerning. Perhaps they all knew something I didn't; perhaps they'd found cause to give the bunker a wide berth and only *I* was stupid and arrogant enough to go stamping through.

I walked down passages dozens of yards long, all of them made of the same painted concrete and each taking me further and further from daylight. A handful of chipped steps here, a slight declivity in the floors there; I knew myself descending, drawing nearer the earth's bosom with every step, and the lower I got, the more prodigious the flooding became. Rooms to the right and left of me, once intended to house nervous doomsday preppers or, really, who could say what, were half-inundated. Well into my journey, I discovered degraded fixtures in some of these rooms—titanic metal objects that the invasive flow had warped beyond recognition. It was the drippage of these that lent the standing water its reddish color and that added to the air that especially nauseating tang of oxidation.

How had Jonah navigated these lengthy passages without a light? I was tempted to put out my flashlight for a moment so that I might acquaint myself with the grade of darkness he'd been forced to grapple with in his wanderings. Pausing in a relatively dry span of corridor, I shut my eyes and found I could imagine it plenty well; his shaky hands against the flaking walls, his feet pattering uncertainly against the concrete and through the occasional standing pool, the sounds of every pace and breath rebounding against the earth and crowding back in on him, just as my own did.

What had begun as an exciting journey into the unknown had quickly transformed into a nightmare. There had likely come a time when, having gone quite deep into the labyrinth, he had walked his fill and wished to return to the entrance, only to find himself marooned in the damp shadows. Always calm and even-keeled, Jonah would not have made a fuss; no, he would not have called out for help or given the rest of us any notice of his troubles. Instead, with a sturdy resolve, he would have done everything in his power to slowly retrace his steps and find his way out.

And in the process, he would only have become more hopelessly lost.

He never *did* make his way out, of course. And when the powers of the above-ground world came looking, they failed to find a scrap of the boy. "So," I asked myself aloud, "what happened, then?"

Frightened and confused, Jonah had eventually wandered into mortal trouble. In the utter blackness of the complex, he could not possibly have known what he was up against, could not have relied on his eyes. And yet, whatever had compelled him to unleash that monstrous scream, it had communicated itself to him without recourse to sight...

But there was nothing in the bunker to fear—nothing that *I* could see, anyhow. The going was thoroughly unpleasant, and in my carelessness I made many opportunities for rude shocks and stoked my own jumpiness. The deep halls were empty, though. I was alone in them, and never once did I doubt that fact as I trudged.

At least, not until I reached the bunker's rightmost extremity.

I had branched off to the right, and though I was astonished at the breadth of the construction, the bunker was not, in fact, endless; I came with little fanfare to a dead end. Narrow doorways appeared to both sides of me, but these would take me no deeper into the earth. Instead, they appeared to lead only into rooms of the aforementioned kind—flooded, filthy, unremarkable spaces the likes of which I'd seen enough of.

I pitched a glance into each of these, and, finding nothing of interest, the entire errand seemed to lose its savor. I had now gotten my fill of adventuring and honestly felt a bit embarrassed at the whole episode. There were finer things for a man of my years to get up to than this. I'd set out in search of catharsis but would leave having found only the stench that now clung to my T-shirt and jeans.

I was turning around, mentally mapping my return to the exit, when I heard something from one of those two back rooms. It was wholly unexpected, and it stopped me in my tracks. My ears were in something of a fog; the constant echoes thrust upon them by the setting had given them a lot to chew on, so at first, I thought they were mistaken. Grinding to a halt and keeping my breath locked in my chest, however, I soon realized that the sound of splashing had been genuine.

From the room on the left, I heard the sound of something slipping into the water.

It had not been a hard or conspicuous sound; rather, it had seemed to me the result of a smooth and practiced movement—a stealthy maneuver. The sound of a crocodile submerging in silent pursuit of its prey was the nearest comparison I could imagine as I stood listening.

And so, naturally, I backtracked. *How strange*, thought I. Perhaps I wasn't so alone in these tunnels after all. A mouse or raccoon, an otter or other creature was sharing the bunker with me and had been spooked into the standing pool by the sound of my advance.

When I returned to the doorway of the room on the left and shone my light in, I found the water disturbed by a series of ripples and a long, shimmering wake. I did not discover an otter there, however—nor a raccoon, a rat, or a crocodile. Even the last would have been far preferable to the thing I *did* find.

I watched as something came floating briskly through the water. *Someone.* Gliding on his back, I saw that it was a boy of roughly twelve. His name was summoned at once to my lips; years and years ago, I'd shouted that same name into this shadowed bunker. His swollen body, wrapped in graying, bulging flesh, was draped in torn jeans and a muddied flannel shirt, and his sandy hair clung to the water's surface like oil. His eyes, greenish-yellow, were open.

More than that, they were fixed on me.

Jonah—or, rather, his corpse—was not merely floating along. With a jerk of his dead limbs, he snapped himself through the water like a great eel and flopped noisily against the floor, mere feet from the doorway. There was a rubbery scrambling; bloated hands pawed against the concrete as he stood and came lurching toward the hall.

My earlier plans were abandoned. Where I had been plotting to carefully retrace my steps and find my way out calmly, I now went barreling down the corridor with the flashlight locked in my fist and my boots thumping out a drum solo. In the off-beats, I could hear his sodden feet squelching in pursuit. A plaintive cry rose up to my back—a voice marred by groaning and disuse but still vaguely familiar to my ear.

"*Wait! Please... don't leave me... Help me find my way out...*"

"Jonah?" I gasped, pausing around the next bend and steadying my light on the path ahead. "J-Jonah? Is that really you?"

"*Please...*" continued my pursuer, "*Please, wait for me. The light... I haven't seen the light in so long...*"

I wasn't in the right headspace for catching up, but I hurled a question into the darkness in spite of myself. "Jonah, what happened to you?"

The corpse's clopping tread was very close now. And so was the groaning voice. "*I got lost. I couldn't see. I've been looking for a way out, but it's too dark. The light... Please, don't take away the light. Please wait for me and help me find my way out.*"

I wanted nothing to do with the hideous thing creeping through the passage behind me, and yet I could not bear the thought of sprinting out and leaving him to howl and weep in the darkness that had kept him prisoner these twenty-plus years. I staggered a little way ahead, but not so far that Jonah would lose sight of my light. "T-There," I continued, "can you see the light?"

"*Yes!*" came the reply.

"Good," said I. "Just keep an eye on it. All right? Follow it, and I'll lead you out of here..." I did not really understand what I was promising, and in the back of my mind, I was reasonably sure that I was hallucinating. What did I expect to do upon reaching the exit with this nightmarish pal in tow? The whole spectacle was absurd enough to make me want to laugh, but the illness stewing in my throat ensured I didn't.

I slowed my pace a touch and held the light high, almost like a torch, so that my old friend could hone in on it like a moth. Together, we walked past innumerable doorways and down many halls in search of the exit. All the while, wracked with pity and nagged by fear, I listened for his tread behind mine. I kept a safe distance, yet never once allowed his footfalls to vanish from my hearing. I had done that, once; I had stood at the threshold with the other kids, listening as his steps died out. I would not do that to him again, however.

Eventually, the rounding of a corner reintroduced me to the main stretch; that is, the initial corridor whose other end was aglow with soothing daylight. Still several paces behind, Jonah took note of the exit, and I heard him sigh with great relief. I put down my flashlight, and together the two of us walked the rest of the way out and strove toward the sun.

We had come very near the exit. I was standing mere feet from the doorway and could feel the warmth of day on my skin. I turned and found Jonah close behind—though, much to my relief, his appearance had reverted to something more familiar. He appeared at my side as a healthy boy of twelve—the way he'd looked the day we'd cycled out to the woods. His smile was broad, his clothes stained only with the grime of boyish recreation. In a word, he was whole again.

The two of us stood for a time in the doorway, peering out into the afternoon and savoring the breeze. After a while, I found the courage to ask him something—something that I and everyone else had long wondered about. "That day, Jonah, when you first went inside..." I glanced back at the long stretch of dark behind us. "What happened?"

"*I started to explore,*" he replied. The recollection quickly chased away his smile. "*I went down the path on the left... and I wandered for quite a while. That's when... that's when something found me in there."*

"Something *found* you?" I asked. "Down the left-hand path, you say? What was it?"

In search of the right words, my friend had been staring silently into the field. Suddenly, he threw a glance over his shoulder, a narrow one, and that was when I heard it.

The *scurrying.*

Something was bolting hard and fast out of the blackness. Flesh rasped energetically against concrete; whether against the floor, walls, or ceiling, I couldn't guess, for the buildup of sound in the passage overwhelmed my senses and inspired visions of numberless grasping limbs. It seemed the sound of a hundred hands, all of them straining to hurl something, some presence, through the shadows.

Whatever moved did not intend to reveal itself; it stopped some distance from the exit, mindful of the daylight. While its bulk remained heaped in shadow, wholly obscure, the thing that it extended toward us—a long, black strand, like a wiry bristle—did not evade my sight. The wiry bristle came shooting out of the depths and, when it touched Jonah's body, I watched him jerk, his eyes widening violently.

Our gazes, together, met just above his navel, where the tip of that wiry line had buried itself. Gore trickled down its length; the black wire remained taut while roaming around in his abdomen. Once it had anchored itself in his organs, he was tugged back into the shadows like a hooked fish. I heard Jonah flop against the floor, heard him writhe as he was dragged hastily into the bunker.

Then came the scream. The *same* terrible scream I'd heard all those years ago, issuing from the *same* place.

And afterward, just like before, the same devilish silence asserted itself.

This time, though, I didn't run straight for town. I hobbled out of the bunker and dropped onto the ground, staring into the doorway. Initially, I stared in disbelief, but the longer I pressed against the darkness of the corridor with my gaze, the more certain I became that I had locked eyes with something unseeable within it.

That was when I finally got up and ran.

———

I'm still convinced it was all a bad dream. Fumes from some underground gas leak, bad air. I haven't told anyone about it because I know they'll have me committed—and, for that matter, I haven't been back home since. I've had to put off my folks several times, declining their offers of get-togethers and meals. They think I'm too much of a city boy now to come visit them, and I'm happy enough to let them believe what they like if it means keeping clear of the woods up north.

The bunker is still out there, and without meaning to I've probably baked enough identifying info into this write-up for you to dig up its precise location and visit it for yourself.

Of course, I'd advise against doing that. No good will come of it. I learned the hard way that, sometimes, the best method of dealing with a traumatic memory is to just leave it alone. So much for *exposure therapy*.

But if you insist on going anyway, make sure to prepare. You'll need a good light. Solid footwear. Don't go at night, either—you'll thank me later.

Oh, and another thing.

Keep to the right; I can't recommend the left-hand path.

THE THING AT THE WINDOW

S HUTTING THE DOOR SOFTLY behind him, he could not shake the stubborn notion that he had been in the motel room once before.

Of course, this was not possible. Only an intoxicating sleepiness could account for such a burst of déjà vu. To his aching and rest-starved eyes, the rumpled twin-sized bed and chipped furniture were familiar friends. The stained lampshade and the dusty curtains seemed the kith and kin of those he'd met in Tacoma just the prior night.

After seventeen hours behind the wheel, his rig flirting constantly with the rumble strips during the last leg, John's mind was filled with many odd things. The flat, twilit scenery had been poisoned by his fatigue. Innocent shadows in nigh-empty fields had struck him as unnecessarily ominous while shuttling his load down the freeway at seventy miles an hour. The side mirrors had been polluted time and again by dark shapes that, after an initial start, proved to be nothing more than spots in his vision.

Having made his delivery, he'd lit out in his cab for the nearest motel, where he'd planned to sleep well and long. He'd cleared the routine with the clerk at the front desk without incident and, within minutes, had been handed his key.

Now, inside the room and wrapped in the stuffy silence particular to rural flophouses, John should have been pleased. Within arm's reach was the bed—the one he'd pined for while slamming gas station coffees on an empty stomach. No roaches had come skittering out when he'd flicked on the light, and turning down the covers, he'd found no bedbugs. The cramped bathroom looked clean and usable enough.

Even so, peace eluded him.

For hours on end, he'd sought a place to lay his head, but having finally arrived, he was gripped by a peculiar restlessness. Fancying himself merely overtired, he sought to soothe his frayed mind by walking slowly around the little room. For a spell, he worked over his face with warm water at the sink and then relieved himself; then, kicking off his boots, he turned on the old television and allowed its murmurings to breathe a little life into the space.

The heaviness in his eyes hadn't abated one iota. His legs were sore after so many hours spent bunched and cloistered behind the wheel, but when he stretched out on the bed, they grew so restless they compelled him back into nervous fits of pacing. He wagered that he'd broken through the worst of his fatigue and was now in the thrall of a most inconvenient "second wind."

A shoeless trip down the main corridor brought him to a trio of humming vending machines, from which came rattling a pitiful dinner of cheese crackers, ginger ale, and chocolate snack cakes. These he brought back to the room, consuming them while pacing the floor and waiting—praying, really—for his aching body to get with the program. If anything, the jolt of sugar only served to waken him further. Drinking down the last of his soda and pitching the crushed can into the little waste bin by the bed, he became conscious of a thunderous beating in his ears: the pounding of his heart.

In his years driving semi-trucks, John had never struggled to sleep after completing a big job. Quite the contrary, it was his custom to sleep like a baby once the goods had been delivered and to spend the following days in a lazy fugue. The alertness that now plagued him, the queer, unsettled feeling that tugged at him every time he tried to shut his eyes, was so utterly beyond the pale that he couldn't help being concerned—and this stress, of course, only riled him further.

Fresh air, maybe—a walk around the remote building—would cure what ailed him. Refastening his boots, John left his room and passed through a glass side door into the parking lot, empty save for a smattering of cars and his own hulking cab. The late September wind carried a chill, yet another stimulus serving to stir his senses where he'd been aiming to quiet them. Hands in his pockets, he crossed the faded blacktop and studied the starless sky. Dim exterior lights haunted the establishment like will-o'-the-wisps, some of them guttering in time with the breeze, and once he'd advanced more than a stone's throw from the side door, their only effect was to blur the borders of the edifice. As he approached the flat, open field beyond the lot and threw a glance over his shoulder, the entire motel seemed a hazy smear on dark glass.

Night insects sang their songs a little further on, their music drifting from patches of overgrowth and from the boughs of rare, slanted trees which grew pell-mell across the murky plain. The thinning leaves of these last went mad with every lurch of the wind, and it was only their rattling that separated him from a perfect and smothering quiet.

It was odd, but the silence, the peacefulness, did nothing to placate him. Instead, it only gave him the space to fixate on a strange notion. John couldn't get away from the feeling that he was being followed. He couldn't guess by whom.

Time and again he nervously plumbed the emptiness, and each time he found nothing. How unsettling it was to feel the presence of another under circumstances so plainly lonesome. This feeling of being carefully tracked by something unseen was not new, however. Behind the wheel of his truck, he'd fallen prey to dreads of the same stripe, seeing things that weren't really there, mistaking shadows and defects in his field of vision for vague phantasms.

John had not been walking long when he lost all faith in his course and began doubling back toward the motel. The longer he trekked beneath the moonless sky, the further he wandered in the shade of sickly trees and kicked at tufts of weed-strangled grass, the more awake he felt.

And more than this, the pressing paranoia he'd been so keen to flee from had not merely followed him out of the stuffy room—it had tightened its grip on him. John found himself many dozens of yards from the edge of the parking lot and was struck by such a foul pang of dread that his step faltered and his dark surroundings seemed to swirl all about him. He felt, in a sense both literal and metaphorical, *exposed* as he stood in the sparse field; felt as though he had put himself in plain view of the very thing his instincts had pressed him to run from.

His bloodshot eyes, though they worked the whole scene over in a panicked fury, could attach no cause to the doom that surged within him. He was alone there, after all—alone as one could be. He had no fear of crickets and katydids, no terror of parked cars or thinning trees. All the same, he felt himself dangerously close to the snare. His was the sense of the doe upon entering the hunter's crosshairs; he awaited only the report of the rifle.

Shuddering against the wind, John lingered dazedly in place, his mind bingeing on doubts and fancies of the most colorful sorts, but still nothing swiped at him from the dark. The only casualty was his hope of a good night's sleep. No matter his earlier exhaustion, a prompt sleep now seemed utterly beyond him.

It was then, while making a final study of the field and attempting to scrounge what little comfort he could from the stillness, that he realized he was not, in fact, alone.

Quite a distance off, from around the trunk of a bent old tree, John spied a white, leering face.

There wasn't light enough for him to be very sure of what he saw, and besides, his mind was already so disturbed at that moment that he should have known better than to take such sights at face value. Nevertheless, as he stood gawking, the pale thing hugging the gnarled shaft of knotty wood looked to him like nothing less than the face of one staring intently in his direction.

He fell back a few paces. *Yes*, it *was* a face—and there emerged now a porcelain hand. It gripped the sinewy bark as though the lurking figure were on the verge of a full reveal.

John was a sensible man, and recalling the frivolous frights he'd weathered on the road just hours before, he groped for sensible explanations. Another motel guest, surely, had decided to go for a short walk, just as he had done. This chance meeting, no matter how unwelcome, was no cause for alarm. Probably the figure in the distance was just as frightened as he was, caught unawares during a peaceful nightly stroll. With this in mind, John sufficiently tamped down his nerves. He took a deep breath and let the tension drain from his bunched shoulders, offering a little wave so as to clear the air and make known his goodwill.

What happened next was no friendly tête-à-tête, no exchange of kindly gestures, but a sudden confirmation that the night's fears were rooted in something very real—something which presently came loping out from behind the slanted tree and across the gloomy field toward him.

Afforded only the scant, ambient light, John watched a tall figure step out from behind the tree—a thing of skeletal thinness, possessed of four willowy limbs and a hairless head. Unclothed and utterly androgynous in overall build, the thing strode forward with its head angled to the right, so that one of its long, bat-like ears was nearly pressed against its heaving shoulder. The face entered into sharper focus with every staggered step; hairless ridges framed small, dark eyes, and the visage terminated in a long, pointed chin. Couched beneath a long, flat nose was a pursed and slender mouth.

Generally manlike in shape, the thing appeared animal in nature. It called to mind a giant bat—though hairless, milk-white, and wingless—and this resemblance was doubly reinforced by the thing's spastic jittering as it stamped across the field. The beady eyes contracted in their little sockets, boring into him from afar, and the thing's colorless lips parted to emit a keening howl.

The very knowledge that he was being seen through those miserable eyes was sufficient to send his blood hiccoughing nervously through his veins. His surroundings, already blurred by darkness, seemed to evaporate completely until his field of vision accommodated only the horror striding toward him. He staggered backward, unable to feel the firm ground beneath his feet.

And then he turned and ran.

A breathless, panicked sprint sent him rocketing across the field and to the cusp of the parking lot, where the smack of his boots against the blacktop jarred him so badly he couldn't keep back a frightened yelp. He quickly reached the side door, and clawing his way in, he bumped against the wall and turned to behold the dim outdoors.

The thing was still there.

It was no illusion, no trick of the light.

Nor had it given up its pursuit. The lanky thing remained on his trail, its willowy form cutting through the blackness and nearing the edge of the lot.

Though John had succeeded in distancing himself, he knew—could *feel*—that its eyes remained upon him. The stare wearied him, sapped his limbs of strength, and it was with no little difficulty that he flopped to his left and came scampering into the front lobby, where the clerk suddenly sat at attention.

"You all right?" asked the man behind the desk, his hand moving discreetly to the phone.

John signaled over his shoulder. "There's something out there, man..." Casting a frightened look through the main doors, he cleared his throat and tried to make himself plain. "Out there, in the parking lot, there's... there's something out there..."

The man behind the desk stood up. "What do you mean?"

"Well, it's a... it's like a monster," he spat, his breathing finally under command.

The clerk smiled uneasily, his gaze divided between the doors and John's pallid face. "Are you... are you *high* or something?"

John shook his head. "No, I mean it. I stepped out for some fresh air, and..."

Slowly, the clerk came out from behind his desk. He sauntered into the lobby proper with his hands on his hips and neared the glass doors, peering this way and that. "Sorry, I don't quite understand. What'd you see, exactly? And where?" He motioned at the threshold. "I don't see anything out there."

"Here," said John, waving him around the bend. "It was out here, by this side door." He shuddered, full in the knowledge that the thing was likely very close now—that it might soon enter the building. He shuffled nervously down the hall and zeroed in on the door, standing to one side so that the clerk might get a look.

Looking rather put-upon, the clerk indulged his frightened customer. He approached the door, rubbing at his stubbled chin while studying the lot and all that lay beyond. When seconds passed without remark, John joined him, and together the pair scanned the darkness for some moments more.

Finally, the desk man let out a long sigh. "Are you sure you're all right?" he asked, turning a critical eye upon him. "There's nothing out there. What did you think you saw? A *monster?*" He added the last with a mocking smirk and a roll of the eyes.

"I'm being serious!" John looked out once again, almost wishing now that the hideous thing would rear its head. Though he stood at gaze, fists balled at his sides, he found only gloom. Gradually, it began to dawn on him that maybe, just *maybe*, he *had* been mistaken—that his tired mind had played tricks on him. Could it have been an illusion? "I'm sorry..." he said. "I was out there, taking a short walk, and I saw the damnedest thing..."

The clerk nodded, not at all convinced, and looked his lodger over in his periphery before taking a last peek out into the night. "Between you and me, you look like you could use some sleep."

John steadied himself against the wall and nodded. "You're right. I'm so tired I must be seeing things." He forced a sheepish smile and broke off in the direction of his room with his head low. "I'm... I'm sorry for the trouble. I'll take your advice and get a little shut-eye."

"G'night, then." At once puzzled and amused, the clerk watched John from the hall until he slipped into his room and shut the door.

Sleep would not so much as shadow John's doorstep.

Earlier, when his paranoia had been little but a vague nuisance, sleep had not come. Now, after his fright in the field, he wasn't sure he'd ever be able to rest again.

Re-entering his room, he'd locked the door but had declined to kick off his boots. A late-night drive to some other motel, far, far from this one, seemed a rather enticing prospect. He walked the floors till he grew dizzy, and several times—when his nerve allowed it—he pulled back the curtains and looked out into the night, searching for signs of the horrific figure in the distance.

He saw nothing, save for the same cars, the same shadows, he'd glimpsed earlier.

"You're tired as hell," he muttered to himself. He brought his palms to his eyes and kneaded at them like a baker. Positioning himself on the edge of the bed, John sought to assess the matter logically. "That thing out there... it couldn't have been real. The guy at the desk was right—you need some sleep, that's all."

There was a substantial wrinkle in John's theory—one that he couldn't easily iron out, no matter what he did. Oftener than not, he was a tired man. On account of his job, his sleep debt was always maxed out, and rare were the days when he felt truly "refreshed." He was familiar, then, with what sleeplessness could do to a tired mind.

Not once had it ever done *that*. The incident in the field was so unlike anything he'd ever experienced. He couldn't simply write it off as an artifact of drowsiness. The thing, staring and malformed, had not come especially close, but even from a distance, he'd judged it to possess the weight and aura of a living, breathing thing. He had heard it howl, and the noise it had made—shrill, grating—had been unlike any other sound he'd ever heard.

But now it was gone.

Again he moved to the window, nudging the sun-faded fabric aside and narrowly scanning the exterior of the motel. There was no sign of it, no sign that anything of note existed beyond the line of darkened cars. From where he stood, the particulars of the field were scarcely visible—too bundled in shadow.

His fatigue was no longer a mental burden alone; his exhaustion was passing into a new and more detestable phase, plaguing his body with all manner of odd aches and numbnesses which rest alone could ameliorate. He stretched out on the bed after making certain that the door and window were locked.

With eyes closed, he endeavored at least to let his body sink into the thin mattress and rest. He shut his eyes, the lids slamming down like heavy doors, and focused on the silence. The lights were on; he'd lacked the nerve to shut them off. The din of the electricity crackling in the walls and the faint settlings of the building were peaceable companions as he tried to settle into dreamless hibernation.

It wasn't long before those eyes snapped open and began restlessly scanning the ceiling. He recalled the thing's misshapen face, the bent and peculiar advance it'd made from behind the gnarled tree. John laughed a little to himself; laughed because it was the only sound he could think to make which might, however slightly, ease his fears.

Probably, by daybreak, he would find it in himself to sleep. The presence of the sun outside his window would chase off all bad thoughts, all vague fears, and he'd finally know rest while the world at large was gearing up for a new morning. Maybe, he thought to himself, he'd even take a much-needed break. He could afford to put off the next job—for a little while, at least. Tourism, much-needed leisure would help him—

Every hair on his body began to levitate. His gaze was drawn to the curtained window, and there it lingered with the weight of a millstone while his heart began inching toward his throat.

There'd been a noise at the window.

It was not a noise he could blame on the wind.

What's more, it was a clear, dry night. Would that he could have steadied himself by accusing a brief drizzle.

It had been a soft tapping sound.

Rap. Rap. Rap.

John waited for what seemed like eons, clutching at the bedspread in the hopes that he'd misheard.

Again, the soft rapping intruded into his room.

Rap. Rap. Rap.

There were no trees outside whose branches might reach the windows, and the bushes growing along the building's perimeter were far too squat to interact with the pane. It could only be the work of something animate, something willful—and in a spasm of terror, he felt quite sure he knew what. Something—*it*—was trying to get his attention.

He ignored the sound. He couldn't have stood up to investigate even had he wished to. Every vital force in him had gelled, rendering him an impotent mass. Even his heart, raucous at the onset, had piped down as if to listen closely, and his blood had stilled in his veins.

Rap. Rap. Rap.

It wasn't going to stop. If anything, the sound was growing in intensity, in vigor—the summons of one who insisted on being acknowledged.

He did not rise from the bed so much as tumble off it, and when he'd found some command of his legs, John passed shakily to the window. A thick silence enveloped all, and for one honeyed moment, he could nearly fool himself into the belief that it was over, that the tapping had ceased and the caller had moved on.

Rap. Rap. Rap.

A long, delirious wait in the room till daylight or an ill-advised glance beyond the curtains. These alone were the paths left to him. So that he might rip off the Band-Aid and perhaps break free of the dread that presently crushed the breath from his lungs, he reached out a stiff hand and chose the latter. The frayed edge of the curtain was pinched; the whole was pulled back in a single, frightened yank.

There are, in times of terror and confusion, occasional lulls—moments when the senses must catch up before ultimate fear or relief can be realized. Upon uncovering the window, John spied in it only the blackness of night. The square frame was outlined in the hazy glow of the light from within his room, and his own dim reflection played there—a whitened mask contorted by anxiety.

Had this emptiness persisted but a second longer, he might've allowed himself the privilege of relaxation, but all hope was promptly snatched away by the large, white hand that suddenly appeared from below and struck the glass.

Smooth, pasty flesh clung to the thin fingers and broad palm. The dark, jagged nails now in view had been responsible for the rapping, and these were slowly, desirously dragged across the glass. Still more of the figure became visible—the milky, crooked arm; the tip of a flabby ear and the crown of a bare, vein-studded head.

Seated beneath the stony brow, the tiny, dark eyes vibrated in their sockets like vermin stirring in their burrows and fixed him with a hatred too awful to be human, yet too plainly malefic to be merely animal. From without, a long wail—the sound, perhaps, of a braking steam locomotive on rusty tracks—pierced the air.

It had arrived.

John flew from the room like a cannonball and went ricocheting down the carpeted hall. He dashed, red-eyed and shuddering, into the lobby, where his fevered charge drew a cry from the desk man's lips. "What the *hell?*"

He screeched to a halt, woozy with dread as he studied the main entrance, and then, like a drowning man, clawed his way to the desk and gripped it like a buoy. "I-I have to go," he choked out. "I need to leave. *Now.*"

"But you've only just—"

"Something's come up," John blurted, his face as white as the floor tiles.

"Your room's already paid for, buddy. I'm not going to refund you for—"

"I don't care about that," John put in. "Please, just... will you walk me out to my truck?"

The clerk furrowed his brow. "You want me to *what?*"

"Just, uh... just come outside with me," John pleaded. "Make sure I get into my cab, that's all..."

The desk man seemed marooned between outrage and pity; he loosed an impatient laugh and came a little way around the desk, sizing up his lodger with a frown. "You're in no shape to drive, man."

John edged his way to the door. "I'm fine," he insisted. "I'm good to drive, believe me. I just need to go. Something's come up, and I have to leave." The closer he got to the door, the further he drew out the clerk from his perch. "Keep an eye on me, will you? From the door, here, at least..."

"Look, I wouldn't—"

Holding his breath, John reached for the door and went bounding into the night like a madman. Certain that death awaited him in the cool night, he raced to avoid its reach and fixed his sights on his cab. The clerk followed him out, muttering the same warnings from the entryway, but his words were whisked away by the steady breeze.

In a shuddering panic, John succeeded in unlocking the driver's-side door. Scurrying into his seat, he immediately brought the truck to life and cut into the gloomy lot with his high beams, where he discovered no trace of the pale, groping fiend. Only the shape of the concerned desk clerk, still waving at him, still mouthing his warnings, came into frame as he panned about, nauseated.

Hands locked tightly around the wheel, John went speeding out of the lot in search of the highway entrance ramp.

There was really no telling how long it'd been on his trail.

He had caught glimpses of it all evening, before he'd even finished making his drop-off. It occurred to him that maybe it'd taken an interest in him even earlier, and as he sped, he racked his mind in search of other oddities that might've been written off as banal in the moment—things sensed but ignored, warnings left unheeded.

The highway opened up before him, a black ribbon threading the seam between unending plains of murk. Signage, rare and scattered, flew by in a blur. John crushed the pedal underfoot, his eyes leaping between the side mirrors and windshield frenetically. Top speed was not fast enough to escape the monstrous thing. Would it be enough for him to cross state lines? To speed into the distance until dawn reared its head? He was moving eastbound, down a carless, lightless stretch, and sunrise was still several hours off.

He entertained thoughts of other motels, many zip codes away. "You could just keep on driving," he told himself, eyeing the fuel gauge. It was nearly full. He could afford to put hundreds of miles between himself and the thing if he so chose.

It was in the right-hand mirror that he first noticed it.

Movement—the creeping progress, maybe, of something at the rear of the cab. John's grip on the wheel faltered, sending the truck listing for a beat.

Something white was clinging to the dusty red body of the cab, barely visible in the corner of the mirror. He could not be sure of what it was. Windblown refuse stuck to the rear panel? An ordinary feature of the rig made strange by the darkness, its proportions overblown by his addled mind?

The rumble strips along the shoulder jostled his attention back to the road. "It's nothing," he told himself through gritted teeth. "You're losing it, man. You're losing it..." Still, when he'd gotten the truck within the lines again, his gaze went drifting back to the mirror, searching out the anomaly once more.

There was nothing there.

The white mass—a curled, gripping hand, he'd feared—was no longer visible. "It was nothing!" he said aloud, cracking a delirious smile. A bit of paper or plastic had clearly been stuck to the rig, and he'd shaken it off. That was all.

Heavy lids beat down upon his blurry line of sight. His arms quaked as he steadied them atop the wheel and slowly cut speed. He began traveling in keeping with the limit for the first time since leaving the motel. He slowed enough, in fact, to read the signs peppered along the road. City names, mile markers, billboards. They all went by like a slideshow.

There arose a sudden *thump* from the top of the cab which robbed him of all control. He leapt up in his seat, the truck swaying as he looked roofward. The blood drained from his face. He was driving through wide, open country, and conditions were clear—nothing, save for a creature scrabbling across the top of the cab, could have produced such a noise, and he knew it.

John hooked a sharp right and then a left; sailing between the lanes, he sought to throw off whatever was clinging to the truck.

But to no effect.

No sooner did he right his course than another *thump* echoed through the cab—and this time, from the uppermost edge of the windshield, a set of pale fingers came into view. Dark claws teased the auto glass as the abomination dragged its weight across the top of the truck and its shadow fell across the hood. In the sparse moonlight, its whole, hideous shape bloomed before him.

It was not the ghoulish, bat-like face that appeared next. Nor did the creature's piercing cry reach his ears as he reared back in his seat.

Instead, the vast, flat edge of a concrete highway divider loomed up before him.

The crunch and whine of twisted metal filled his ears as the front end disintegrated.

The lonely stretch of highway flashed red and blue. An ambulance had sidled up to the wreckage, but the gurney in its rear remained empty while the paramedics tried to decide which piece of the victim to load first.

A highway patrolman waved on a slow-moving gawker in a sedan before crossing the lanes. He paused beside the wreck, wincing a little as he took in the mangled chassis. "Hell of a mess," he uttered.

The punished driver's-side door had been wrenched open, allowing the paramedics a measure of access to the interior, and one of them, with a heavy sigh, hopped back onto the asphalt. "I don't get it. He had to have been going well over the speed limit to crash this hard. Was he suicidal?"

The patrolman shook his head. "No, you see this all the time with these guys. I bet he fell asleep behind the wheel and didn't know what hit him."

The paramedic took a deep breath and scanned the dark plains. "There must be a dozen different motels within miles of here. Why not just grab a room and rest up?" Perhaps it was only an effect of the flashing lights, but while trawling the distance, he thought he detected movement—a vague stirring in the darkened field.

He had only to blink and it was gone. Stillness prevailed. The paramedic wiped at his eyes with the back of his gloved hand. "Guess I'm not one to talk, though. I need to get some sleep myself."

DIAPHANOUS

PEYTON CLUTCHED THE CAMOUFLAGED netting to himself and turned a wide eye to the vast wall of woods at his back. For some time he'd been engaged in this obsessive surveillance of the shadowed forest, awaiting some fright, some material horror, which never reared its head. His thin neck forced his eyes round into another lap, and he found himself gazing for the thousandth time at the tapestry of leaves and shrubs and wild grasses. My partner, gaunt and grizzled after nearly fourteen days lost in the wilderness, then spoke for the first time in what must have been hours.

The two of us had long since abandoned the practice of idle chatter; to speak was to forego listening, and in these damned woods, not nearly so empty as they appeared by day, hearing proved more valuable a commodity than cheerful talk. Thus, to my mind, the breaking of this carefully cultivated silence promised a disclosure, an insight, of real value.

"We're being watched, Frank. I can feel their eyes upon us now," said Peyton, whiskers crawling across his cheeks in a tight wince. "This camouflage... our attempts to be silent... It's all meaningless. They know we're here, Frank. And they're watching."

Many hours had passed since I, too, had last spoken anything more than a grunt or groan, and when I found my voice there, seated by the water's edge, my reply was scalding. I was angry not simply on account of his paranoia, or because I hated the shakiness and timidity that'd possessed him over the course of the preceding days, but because he had shattered our precious silence to note something I knew well enough myself. "*Of course* they're watching, you idiot!" I spat under my breath. "We haven't got an hour of daylight left. Things are stirring, coming to in the woods, which were sluggish at the height of day. Keep your mouth shut. They'll hear us!" I warned. "They'll hear us!"

My calloused hands, blackened by days of wandering, tightened around my scrap of camouflage netting—the sole souvenir of the camp we'd abandoned tens of miles away on that moonlit night. Instinctively, the two of us had clung to the stuff—had gone even to the trouble of dividing it into two equal portions—that we might drape ourselves in it and disappear into the natural scenery. While trekking along the endless shore or taking our rest, we huddled beneath the textured netting like humps of cowardly moss.

There are things in this world that cannot be so easily fooled, however. The senses of these are not limited to base sight, hearing, and taste. Their perceptions are filtered through a more panoramic array and enjoy far greater precision than those of humble man.

It was a thing of *this* kind—neither man, nor animal—that held us in its gaze from somewhere in the forest.

This was the same gaze we'd been running from for almost fourteen days.

We had been drawn to this wild country, just like those who'd come before us, by the promise of gold. That our predecessors in the chase had either vanished or died under mysterious circumstances did not deter us in the least; in fact, the two of us, boasting a combined three decades of experience in hiking and general bushcraft, haughtily noted the failures of the others and drew up new, better routes for our expedition, which would take us deeper into the so-called "Headless Valley" than anyone had gone before. Our kit had been state-of-the-art. We'd fancied ourselves strong and capable.

Neither had the two of us been deterred by the illegality of our quest. Large swaths of the region had been locked down in decades prior by conservationists on both the provincial and federal levels, making our search for gold all the riskier. If caught, heavy fines or imprisonment surely awaited us. To venture is sometimes to gain, though; depending on how the coin-toss went, we would either emerge felons or Croesuses, and fancying ourselves cleverer than the sleepy mounted police, we ultimately banked on our coming out the latter.

The two of us stepped into our boat and plunged into the choppy waters of the South Nahanni. It is a volatile river on the best of days, at turns glassily calm and violently turbulent, snaking for untold miles between towering ramparts of mountain. Even in full sun, one may sail for hours in the shade of these mountains, which crowd upon the water from both sides and choke the valley of light. As such, the drink is always cold, the rare strips of habitable bank are invariably damp, and night often brings with it rolling waves of mist.

By day, we navigated rapids and strove toward the heart of this northwestern territory more than eleven-thousand miles square. Our nights were spent on the banks of the river, where we pitched our tents, tracked our progress on maps, and supplemented our simple meals with local fish. In spots where the waters were shallower and stiller, we made liberal use of our sluices, dredging up loads of stinking sediment in search of gold.

I recall the day we were treated to our first taste of the stuff. Parked on a slender patch of shore some fifty miles deep, our panning turned up a wedge of gold the size of my thumb. At its discovery the two of us rejoiced like madmen, our cries bouncing off the gray mountain walls. Further investigations of the riverbed proved fruitless, but Peyton and I, both, were convinced that the mother lode would be found just a little further downstream.

And in the days that followed, our conviction seemed on the verge of being borne out. Subsequent efforts brought up smatterings of gold—a dime-sized piece here, a handful of glimmering pebbles there. All were tucked lovingly into a reinforced sack, to be divided equally and sold off at journey's end. With every ounce we added to the sack, our ambitions and fantasies grew wilder, more insatiable. I remember now—not without some bitterness—that we would sit along the bank, eating grilled pike by the fire, dreaming almost until dawn of the high life.

In the end, however, the Nahanni Valley got to keep its gold. The aforementioned sack was among the many essentials we abandoned in fleeing our camp. We lost our tents, sluices, rifles, and other supplies, too.

I wish that I could explain what it was that drove the two of us—able-bodied, experienced, and greed-possessed men—to flee the camp and to abandon all we held precious. Only mortal terror, perhaps, could have seen to such a thing; and, certainly, one must be very frightened indeed to attempt navigation of the rapids in pitch darkness as we did. Our escape had been little better than a suicide attempt, but instinctively Peyton and I had thought it better to perish at the hands of nature than to fall prey to the things we met by the treeline.

The night our expedition broke down—the night we threw away our lofty plans and centered ourselves strictly upon the objective of survival—was a very pretty one, in retrospect. Though the walls of the valley served to choke out the light, our camp that night happened to enjoy just such a placement as to invite bands of steady moonglow. We could see one another clearly even when the fire was low, and were able to gaze a little distance into the thick wood that grew from the mountainside. The edge of the water was lent a dazzling shimmer, and the mist rolling across our camp shone like diamond dust.

Even hardened and avaricious men can appreciate beauty; we lounged by the water's edge and soaked it all in. We shared a simple meal, studied the glowing treeline before us, and traced the movement of small animals in the wood as we dreamt about our impending wealth. We spied many a bat circling the treetops in search of food, and glimpsed our fair share of red foxes and otters. Had the moonlight not been so generous, we would have missed out on seeing all of these.

We would have missed out, too, on seeing the thing which drew Peyton's eye and made him sit up, his face going almost as pale as the moonlight.

I didn't notice my partner's reaction; not at first. By the time I'd emerged from my thoughts and asked him some idle question, he'd gone totally pale and wide-eyed, so that I initially thought him ill. "What's the matter?" I asked him. "You feeling sick?"

In answer, Peyton raised a shaky finger and thrust it toward the treeline.

I wasn't immediately sure what he was pointing at. The region is home to wolves, coyotes, grizzlies, and other creatures that do not make particularly friendly guests, but I found none of these as I sat up and scoured the treeline. "Well?" I whispered. "What is it, man?"

He was slow in answering. "T-There, in the t-trees," he finally stammered. His finger, still extended, jabbed at the air like a lance. "You see that?"

"See what?"

"I think... it's watching us, Frank..." He suddenly withdrew his finger, thinking better of pointing *it* out.

A little irate, I rose up with a groan, dusted myself off, and went traipsing past the fire toward the trees, eager to figure out what had him so spooked. I didn't make it two paces from Peyton's side, my eyes scouring the wood, before I suddenly retreated half a dozen paces. In fact, I kept on backing away until my boots met the soggy bank of the Nahanni.

The two of us *were* being watched by something in those woods. Peyton had not been mistaken. Precisely *what* was doing the watching, though—this was a question which neither of us could answer.

I know a bear when I see one. I know mountain lions and bison, moose, deer, the whole lot—and I know a man when I see one, too. The thing in the woods was none of these. It had no fur, no bared fangs or ready antlers, no claws... For that matter, it didn't possess anything like a body at all.

Huddled between a mass of knotty pines was a whitish, misty silhouette; a pale figure. It hadn't jumped out at me from the first glance on account of its delicacy, its—if you can excuse me for using such a ludicrous word—*ethereal* quality. There was no *physical* body there, exactly, just a white, vaporous impression of one, as though the light fog had become snagged on a tree limb and had twisted into a semi-human shape.

I took it for nothing but an uncanny illusion perpetrated by the fog and moonlight working in union. When the initial shock had passed, I firmed up a little and was ready to dress down my companion for having been so easily taken in.

But then the thing took a step.

Nigh bodiless, the vapor-wrapped thing drew nearer. Pulling away from the shadows of the wood as it did, more of its glimmering, translucent outline was bared to the moon and rendered diaphanous. It was like looking at a densely woven cobweb, in some ways—a human outline in gossamer. Expressionless—that is, entirely without features—the cloudy presence was nonetheless engaged in careful study of our camp; it faced us with a certain brazenness, leaned like an eavesdropper.

In this land of bears and wolves, I was never very far from my rifle, and this I fetched up from the fireside while keeping the apparition in view. "W-Who goes there?" I shouted, seeking to draw the thing out. Though my heart raged in my chest and Peyton looked ready to bolt from the camp altogether, I assuaged myself with reasonable inner talk. This was no phantom, no "spirit" or anything of the kind. We had come upon some camper, some vagrant, some well-meaning native, probably... Though this stretch of country was renowned for its emptiness, it had been explored by many prior to our visit. Our odds of encountering another human being in so remote a corner were mighty low, but they were not zero, after all.

My challenge was answered in an unexpected way while Peyton knelt by the fire, shuddering. With the butt of my rifle pressed to my shoulder, I made a great show of taking aim—but I was quickly put off from the task by the emergence of a second figure, very similar to the first. Another white, gaseous thing came sneaking out of the trees, its wavering outline caught by the pale moonlight. Taken off guard, I lowered my rifle and peered at my companion. It had been my intention to ask him if he, too, had seen this second figure, but before I could spit out the question, a voice came ringing out of the woods and sent a jolt through us both.

"I tell you, this is a literal goldmine we're sitting on. We're about to knock it wide open, Peyton, and when we do our grand-children's grandchildren will be well taken care of!"

Peyton and I both blanched, and for a dread moment we locked eyes.

The voice from the woods was *mine.* In pitch and cadence, in the faint pauses and hints of giddy laughter, the utterance was unmistakably mine. These words, however, had not been on my lips for some minutes; I had spoken them earlier in the night, while the two of us had been conversing over dinner. Now, they were being thrown back at me from the virgin wood; an echo several minutes delayed.

"The first thing I'm going to do when we're clear is find myself a wife—or several! What do you think, Frank? A harem of blondes?"

Peyton squeezed a handful of wet sand hard enough to make a diamond when his own words came tumbling out at us.

"Ah, why not a few brunettes, too? A man ought to diversify his fortunes!"

The sound of our chuckling filled the trees and washed against the high mountain walls; the same laughter we'd shared while stoking the fire just minutes prior.

Our entire fireside chat was being replayed—performed—by something in the dark woods. It was chilling enough for us to realize that our talk had reached other ears in this wilderness, that we'd been listened to, but the *most frightening* aspect of it all was easily the quality of the imitation.

The party responsible had attained a *perfect* mimicry of us both.

Though I still held my gun, I suddenly couldn't remember how to work it. The thought of intimidating the figures, of firing a warning shot, didn't cross my mind—I must have known in my gut that such measures would amount to nothing. By all appearances, the things in the woods were not flesh-and-blood organisms, but mere hallucinations—knots of fog tied into odd shapes by the faint breeze. I simply stood frozen, watching the hazy duo as they watched us.

Peyton, though, wasn't able to sit still. He immediately went groping for the bank, and I heard him *thump* into the boat as he rolled it over and prepared to set sail. "F-Frank, come on!" he insisted. "We have to get out of here!"

I was afraid, make no mistake, but I was not yet at the point of abandoning our camp. What's more, I knew just how dangerous the river would be by night. Though some portions were shallow and calm, the rapids further on would prove an almost insurmountable challenge to us in the dark. "What do you think you're doing? Get out of that boat, you imbecile! You trying to kill yourself?"

Peyton gripped the oar and threatened to launch without me. "Suit yourself, Frank, but I'm getting out of here!"

"Wait! Don't—"

There was a great splash as the boat hit the water.

And that wasn't all.

Suddenly, the two white figures in the woods were on the move. Marching on legs of swirling fog, the semi-transparent things came bursting out of the shadows and made straight for our camp. A distance of mere yards separated me from them, and as they closed the gap, they drifted in and out of my sight. When the moonlight hit them full on, they wore it like a flowing shroud; fog clung to them so closely that a vague outline became clear through the rippling tongues of mist, an outline suggestive of grinning skulls, of stick-thin limbs and grasping, skeletal digits. But when the moon was not upon them, they moved through the mist completely unseen—were blanketed with it as though it were snow. As such, their progress toward the bank proved astonishingly rapid. Each time they disappeared from view for a breathless moment, they would surface much nearer at hand.

The things had drawn very near indeed when I lost my nerve and went galloping into the boat. I dropped my rifle on the way, and in my panic did not think to recover it. Tramping into the shallows, I clawed my way into the boat and watched as Peyton worked the oar in a fury, sending us at once down the dark river. While he gouged the water like a madman, I righted myself and fixed my gaze on the shore we'd fled. Our fire still flickered, and our tents, filled not only with our treasure but with the stuff of our survival, remained pitched along the waterfront.

Standing on the edge of the bank, too, were a pair of white silhouettes. The things hovered there, watching, as if they'd come to see us off. Eventually they became one with the fog, buried in it, but the weight of their scrutiny persisted for a long while.

Five, ten minutes later, we found a bend in the river and our camp was blotted from sight entirely. We had made our escape.

What the figures had intended for us, if anything, was a mystery; frankly, we were very glad to live in ignorance of their purpose.

Some time later, Peyton finally cut speed and allowed the natural current to do its work. At this point, fairly removed from the camp, there was no great sigh of relief between us, no chatter of what we'd seen. Bathed now in the syrupy shadows of the Nahanni Valley, we heard the distant rush of rapids and knew that we were soon to do battle with the river in almost complete darkness. We sat, the two of us, and I took up the second oar. As we approached the nighted rapids, our silence was that of prisoners led to the guillotine.

There is little use in my embellishing the facts, or in giving a very thorough rundown of what happened next.

Suffice it to say, we lost our fight against the South Nahanni. The boat capsized and was lost to us; somehow, though, we remained afloat in the punishing flow long enough to grasp at a chunk of crumbling shoreline. We did not die that night, but as we crawled up onto the banks, shivering and sodden, we wished, perhaps, that we had.

We flopped onto dry land like two seals, panting and cursing. Sense was slow in returning to us, but when it did, we began to realize just how desperate our situation now was. We had no food on us, nor any means of catching any. We had knives in our pockets, and I had a large scrap of camouflage netting on my person. There was nothing else. No maps, no compass, no guns—and, perhaps worst of all, no boat.

As best we could guess, we'd gone two or three miles from the camp in total. Apart from the possibility that the abandoned site was still haunted by the misty things, the two of us knew that we could not backtrack even if we wished to. The rapids were far too strong; we could never hope to swim against them, and what's more, the gaps in the shoreline were such that we could not make an approach by land. Our camp and all of our belongings were lost to us. We knew it at once, and were forced to make peace with it.

While wringing out our clothing and attempting a small fire for the sake of warmth, we finally got around to discussing the fright that'd propelled us down the river—and not without many nervous glances upstream.

"What do you think that was?" I asked Peyton while emptying my boots of water.

He did not feel imaginative enough to hazard a guess, and only replied, "Do you think we lost 'em?" He paused. "Do you think... they'll follow us?"

Desperate to build up my partner, I took it upon myself to play the strong man. "No, we've seen the last of them. I'm sure of it."

Through great effort, we finally got our fire going. Physically and mentally exhausted, we slept around it like cavemen—albeit lightly, and with frequent awakenings. Still shaking off our dread, the two of us spoke very little in the hours that followed, and our ears made much of the smallest sounds. The faintest rustling awoke in us truly primal terror; any perceived deviation from the sounds of nature saw us both sitting bolt upright, pale-faced and wide-eyed. Every time, these reactions of ours were in vain.

Except for one.

I stood relieving myself a few hours before dawn, and moved to check the dryness of my boots by the fire when the hairs on the back of my neck suddenly stood at attention. Peyton, snoring uneasily up to that moment, quieted and shortly awoke, his eyes blinking in apparent confusion and his heavy head on a swivel. Though dozing, his senses, too, had picked up on something in our immediate surroundings. Together, we crouched by the fire and looked out across the river. We took in the mountain walls and the chaotic sprawl of pines that grew alongside them. We studied the great stones that jutted here and there from the moist earth, and the muddy bank of the river, which still bore the deep gouges we'd made in our hasty clambering.

Nothing looked awry. Our eyes met only the natural world.

It was our ears that first alerted us to the presence of a threat.

From some shadowed corner in a nearby copse—Peyton and I could not agree precisely where—we heard voices engaged in strained conversation.

"*What do you think that was?*" said the one.

After a long pause: "*Do you think we lost 'em? Do you think... they'll follow us?*" chanced the other.

"*No,*" said the first, with a puffed-up bravado that could not but ring hollow in my ear, "*we've seen the last of them. I'm sure of it.*"

My blood, as well as Peyton's, froze.

Our makeshift camp was awash in deep shadow. Thinking back to our encounter upstream, I knew that the misty things could not be seen in the dark; only in the moonlight did they give the faintest evidence of their presence. Thus, I understood immediately that the things were upon us, that they had followed our progress downriver, and that they had sat quietly by, listening from the shadows.

We did not give them an opportunity to step out of the mist and dark, but instead threw on our soggy boots and fled. We abandoned a second fire—our only source of comfort in the wretched wilderness—and went shambling through the brush for what must have been another two miles. All the while, we threw our gazes backward, fearing what the moon might show us.

Eventually, the horizon lightened and, mercifully, the light of day was poured out upon us. We erupted onto a sandy bank and collapsed, praying for an end to the night's pursuit. Some nervous hours ticked by before the two of us, much reassured by the brightness and warmth, decided that we had properly escaped. By the afternoon, we grew bold enough to place our focus on survival, and we did our best to chart a course back to civilization without recourse to the usual instruments.

In the daylight, the terror of the previous night seemed to us a dream, a shameful hallucination. We laughed about it while enjoying the sun's favor.

Later, when the sky began to darken and the valley dimmed, we could no longer find it in ourselves to laugh, however.

And now, having repeated the cycle of terrified flight for almost fourteen nights running, Peyton and I are at wit's end. Our primitive traps have brought us very little food, and though our forays into the woods have been many, we've come away with almost nothing edible. Growing feebler by the minute, gaunt and achy, we watch from the river's edge as the sun dips out of the sky.

Peyton, face upturned, looses a great sigh and whispers to me, "I don't know how much longer we can keep this up. The river goes on and on. I know our plan is to follow it, but…"

"It's the only landmark we can trust," I put in soothingly. "If we stray much from the river, we could wind up marooned in the wilderness. If we follow its flow, however, we'll eventually meet with civilization. It's only a matter of time."

"Yes," he replies, watching with trembling lips as the sky begins to darken in earnest, "but time is the one thing we haven't got, Frank. Tonight, any minute now, they'll be—"

I stop him with a fierce glance. "Enough. Enough of this defeatist talk," I demand. "They can't follow us forever, you hear me? Sooner or later, we'll give them the slip."

"Do you really think they'll leave us alone?" he asks like a frightened child.

"Yes. Yes, I do. Please, put them out of your mind. They'll give up. I know they will."

Peyton is heartened by this, nods, and nestles more deeply into the netting.

Night falls. Thick silence grows up between us until only the current and the breeze and the rare night bird can be heard. The night is warmer; we don't bother with a fire. We're hoping to move at first light—and that, soon, we'll come upon a house, a building, some sign of civilized life...

I'm startled from my brooding when Peyton suddenly speaks up. *"Do you really think they'll leave us alone?"* he asks, tone wavering as if on the verge of tears.

Anger wells up in me, and I turn to him with balled fists. "Didn't I just tell you to stop worrying?"

But Peyton isn't looking at me, and his lips are glued shut in a quivering scowl. He's turned around completely, and is staring wide-eyed into the wall of trees and mist behind us.

It's time to run.

Famished legs are made to sprint, and the two of us bolt downstream with our heads low. Slipping through banks of fog and hopping past outcroppings of stone, we trace the river's edge as closely as we can. The new moonlight is parceled out by the miserly valley; at one point, I nearly lose my footing and tumble into the water. Peyton smashes his already shaky knee against the trunk of a fallen tree, and only by pure adrenaline does he keep limping along behind me.

Our flight is haunted not simply by the white figures in the mist, but by the knowledge that death is likely the only form of escape open to us. This wild territory has consumed us; there is nothing for miles upon untold miles, and despite my assurances to the contrary I know how isolated we are. Starvation or wild animals will claim us if the things in the shadows do not. Civilization lies far, far from our grasp; it is unlikely we will ever see another human being again.

But what's *this!?*

Peyton and I glimpse a flickering light in the distance, a warm orange glow that cuts through the fog and dark. It is the inviting light of a lit hearth, perhaps, or a farmer's evening bonfire. Maybe it's a camp of local Indians. Powered now by hope and all the joy that comes with it, we charge on down the bank toward the light—our sole salvation.

We are very near the source of the glow now, and we're close enough to see it for what it is: a modest campfire. Though still a good distance off, shadows shift around it; shadows indicative of a small presence. The fire's makers are seated around it, undoubtedly kicking back and enjoying the warmth. Peyton and I dash toward them, ready to cry out in thankfulness and desperation, and the outline of the camp comes into sharper focus.

And it is then, as the layout of this camp enters fully into view, that our rickety feet lose their pacing and we stumble to our knees some yards from the ring of firelight.

There are two men seated by the fire; jovial, carefree men, they cast long shadows across the river. Their tents are stationed close to the waterfront, each boasting a few panels of camouflage netting. Moonlight floods their simple camp; ribbons of the stuff come pouring through a ridge in the mountain walls.

The first man, finishing the last of his grilled pike, says, "*I tell you, this is a literal goldmine we're sitting on. We're about to knock it wide open, Peyton, and when we do our grandchildren's grandchildren will be well taken care of!*"

The other, peering up into the night sky, says, "*The first thing I'm going to do when we're clear is find myself a wife—or several! What do you think, Frank? A harem of blondes?*"

"*Ah, why not a few brunettes, too?*" quips the first one. "*A man ought to diversify his fortunes!*"

Together, the pair of campers chuckle heartily.

I feel my heart writhe and sputter. My companion is swooning; he's on all fours, panting in the grass.

Somehow, we've returned to our camp.

Those tents are *our* tents.

Those words are ours, too. The voices are *just right*.

But the two men seated there are *not* us.

Both campers stiffen.

They know we're there—that we're watching—and they start to turn around, real slow.

Two faces are half-revealed by the firelight; white, cadaverous. A thread of white mist tours an empty socket like an eel. Coils of vapor come rolling out of an empty mouth and mingle with the smoke.

Suddenly, Peyton looses a little laugh beside me—a nervous, unhinged kind of sound forced past a blubbering sob. "S-Say," he whispers to me. "They look like a friendly lot. Maybe w-we should ask them for directions..."

Morel Season

THE MUSHROOM MERCHANT MEANDERED up the side road, basket in hand. The man—Elliott, he was called—had been painted a crisper shade of brown since he'd last been sighted, which could only mean that his explorations of the region's wilds had deepened. Rough-cut and middle-aged, ropey as a stray dog, Elliott's sandy smile was an ugly thing to behold—a broad showcase of oddly spaced teeth and fat tongue. The man's nose was as broad and flat as the mushrooms he sometimes peddled, and the young chef, watching him traipse northward with many tips of the hat to those he passed, had long believed him to be a former prizefighter.

"What've you brought me today?" asked the chef, helmer of a modest restaurant called La Brasserie. He looked the seedy mushroom slinger up and down, meeting the unsightly smile with one of his own. "It's late in morel season, Elliott. I can't imagine the hunt has been particularly fruitful these last few days."

A thick, ruddy finger found its way to the tip of Elliott's newsboy cap as he drew near. "Then you are lacking in imagination, chef! Look here, a bounty!" A basket draped in brown cloth was hefted forth with a grunt and set down on the pavement before the chef.

Half in disbelief, the cook dropped to one knee and pulled away the covering, revealing a mound of wild mushrooms—things of startling size and an impossible-to-fake freshness. "How in the world?" he muttered, rifling through the haul with wide eyes. There were chanterelles aplenty, the odd lion's mane and chaga, too. White buttons made up the largest portion, but appearing in their midst were not a few prime morels, and these were plucked up covetously for closer inspection. "I can't understand it. The season's all but over, Elliott! Where did you find these?"

"Trade secret," replied the peddler with a shrug. "I have my sources, Nicholas. I have my sources."

"I'll say you do. You've just been to the local supermarket, haven't you—and you're fixing to sell me refrigerated imports at a markup!"

"Do those look like imports to you, chef?" asked Elliott. "I bring you these delicacies from our native soil. The yield of my day's labor! Of course, if you aren't interested, one of the other Michelin hopefuls in town will surely bite."

"Nonsense." Nicholas went rifling through his chef's whites and revealed a billfold. Peeling a few greenbacks from it, he stuffed the funds into the peddler's loamy palm and took possession of the basket. "I don't know how you do it, but one of these days you *must* tell me where you're finding these, Elliott. I have to know."

"Oh?" replied the man with another tip of the hat. "Are the owners giving you days off now, chef?"

"Hardly," said Nicholas with a sigh. "But one of these evenings, perhaps, after the dinner service, I'll have you over for a drink and you can tell me all about your choicest honey holes."

"Ah, so that you can send one of your sous-chefs into the wild and cut me out of the equation?" Elliott stuffed the cash into his pocket and pulled away with a chuckle and a wave. "Not on your life, chef. Now, you'd best get back to the kitchen. I fear the consommé is boiling over!"

The weekly ritual came to an abrupt end. The mushroom hawker went shuffling from the curb, tipping his hat at passersby as he went, and turned a corner.

Armed now with the freshest mushrooms money could buy, the young chef threw open the back door of La Brasserie and tossed the teeming basket onto the back counter. He and his staff would now go about preparing them for the evening's guests—guests he hoped would include Michelin inspectors.

The restaurant's unexpected closure on Saturday evening came down to sheer bad luck. A powerful storm that morning had knocked out the power in every building within a few miles of La Brasserie. When the fridges ceased to hum and their contents began to spoil, Nicholas salvaged what he could and fixed an impromptu meal for the staff on the gas range. The place was thoroughly cleaned during the daylight hours, and plans were made to reopen on Monday.

It was in the later stages of arranging this temporary shutdown, while the tired cooks were considering an indulgent trip into the wine cellar in the interest of broadening their palates, that Nicholas spied the reedy mushroom seller coming down the drag. He carried nothing in his ruddy hands this day, and though he passed others on the street, he gave no tip of the cap. Instead, he walked with his head low and fists in his pockets, grumbling to himself. He had come within a dozen yards of La Brasserie's back door when he suddenly began scanning the restaurant's facade and locked eyes with the idling chef who'd stolen out for a smoke break.

Nicholas ashed his cigarette and met the mushroom peddler with a nod. "How goes it, Elliott? I didn't expect to see you here today. Anyway, we've had to shut down on account of the storm. No power for blocks around. Come by Monday with more of those morels—if you can find 'em."

Elliott's smile was no prettier than usual, but it *was* significantly more strained. "Good evening, chef," he said, sniffing the misty air. "Sorry to hear about the power outage. Can't imagine that's good for business." He cast his rheumy eyes upon the other cooks in the vicinity; a few were still carrying bins of spoiled ingredients to the dumpsters, while some were leaning against the restaurant's brick facade with their sleeves rolled up and cigarettes between their fingers. The wandering peddler seemed in want of privacy, for he dropped his tone considerably as he went on and watched the others keenly, as if to ensure the narrowest possible audience for what followed. "I came to talk mushrooms, as a matter of fact. But not to sell you any..."

Nicholas took a long drag, his brow arched. "How do you mean, Elliott?"

"You're always going on about it. '*Where do you find these mushrooms?*' Well, chef, I thought I'd come by today and give you a peek behind the curtain, so to speak." Elliott cleared his throat. Pulling his knotted fists from his pockets, he crossed his arms and took to pacing. "You see, I've found something today. Something very special, I believe. And I'd like your professional opinion on it."

The chef dashed his cigarette out against the heel of his shoe and flicked the butt away. "And what might that be? Weren't you telling me just last week that your honey holes are a trade secret?" He grinned, trying to lighten the mood. "I'd hate to cut into your profits."

Elliott was in no laughing vein, though, and his flat, pugilist's nose wriggled as he drew in a deep breath through wide nostrils. "I went out late this afternoon," he began, "just an hour or two after the last drops fell. It was a new spot. You know, I like to explore. I pushed into a woodland about twenty minutes east of here...

"Well, Nicholas, I found something. Something, I think, that's rather special. But... I don't quite know what to make of it." Elliott sighed. "I've been in this business since I was a lad. My uncle taught me. You know how it is that I always deliver the goods? *That's* how—it's been passed down over generations. And you, more than anyone, would agree that I know my stuff, yes?"

Nicholas put up no resistance to the claim. "Your knowledge of fungi is sound, Elliott. You're good at what you do."

"So imagine my surprise, then, when I stumbled upon something I couldn't identify today."

With a furrowed brow, the chef shook his head. "A mushroom? Something out of the ordinary?"

Elliott elaborated, his hands working in a frenzy of gesticulation. "They're morels—or something *very* close to morels, all right? The colors are... *peculiar*, though. Not like anything I've ever seen. I've been bringing you the usual browns, the occasional whites. These, though, are black and red. Almost glittering..."

"Could be a false morel, something poisonous," put forth the chef.

"No chance," the mushroom peddler shot back. "I know a false morel when I see one. This is something else. I believe that I've happened upon a new variety of morel, Nicholas. They're larger than any I've seen previously, and I think that they could be truly delicious. What's more... I've found them growing in great abundance... but only in this particular locale." He lifted his cap and raked at his thinning hair before plopping it back down again. "Such a thing, you understand, would be of great interest in the culinary world. A new variety of mushroom—something sumptuous and exotic—could really set a young chef apart, no?"

"I see what you're doing," replied Nicholas. "How much are you looking to charge me for the privilege?"

"Not a dime," came the rejoinder.

"You're running a charity now?"

"I'm simply curious, Nicholas. I don't know precisely what I've found, so I can't in good conscience charge you for it. You've been a solid customer of mine for some time, and so I came to you first. If you would be so good as to join me on a walk to the spot in question, we could harvest some. Then, with your skill, you could cook them up for us, bring out the best in them. Once we've tasted them, we can decide what they're worth—if they have a place on a world-class menu."

"It's generous of you," said the chef. He turned to the sky and found its hazy grays still alight with the glow of a waning sun. "We might have an hour or two of light yet. Is that enough time, though?"

"Yes, yes, I reckon so," replied Elliott. "If you're free, that is." He glanced at the other staff still loitering by the back entrance.

"On any other day, I would have had to decline. Today, though, you've caught me at a good time." Removing his apron, Nicholas approached his sous-chefs and passed on a few instructions to ensure a smooth closing. Then, fetching his keys and jacket from the back room, he rejoined Elliott on the street. "It'll be faster if we drive. Tell me whereabouts we're headed," he said, seeking out his sedan along the main drag.

Traffic proved very sparse on account of the day's ill weather, allowing the duo to make brisk progress down abandoned country roads and through rain-swept fields. Nicholas was urged onto a hilly eastern expanse by his fidgeting passenger, and in the space of ten minutes they found themselves navigating a commotion of greenery punctuated only by their narrow strip of road. While riding the gentle inclines and drops, the two of them puffed at cigarettes, windows open.

Neither, however, said anything until the car came to a stop upon a grassy shoulder at Elliott's urging. The two men, mere acquaintances for some months, suddenly found themselves alone on a lonesome avenue, and the suspicions of both seemed mildly pricked by the sudden increase in their involvement. Elliott, taking many a nervous drag from his smoke, had traded his usual congeniality for something more tentative. He seemed most uncomfortable in the passenger seat, fidgeting like a man plagued by guilt or wearied by the weight of deception. The chef, for his part, wondered just how trustworthy the mushroom-slinger was—whether he had done a foolish thing in accompanying him to so remote a locale.

When the car was parked, Elliott hastily undid his seatbelt and stepped out. Nicholas followed, locking the doors and tugging on the waistband of his slacks. They had made it to a lush patch of street-side growth which gave way to numberless towering trees. The day's storm had done a number on these woods, downing a profusion of branches and leaving the ground itself not a little murky. Elliott, already dressed in mud-stained boots, thought nothing of these conditions and went ambling from the road toward the treeline.

Nicholas, having come this far, fell into step behind him. "So, what're we looking for, exactly?" he asked, intruding upon the songs of evening birds.

"There's a spot a little ways in," explained the ruddy guide. He pawed at his whiskered cheeks as he went stomping between the trees, his gaze narrow.

"How'd you find it?"

Elliott shook his head. "I was meandering, as one does, and happened upon that little shoulder back there."

"On foot?"

"I was walking off a bender. I spent the night drinking and only started sobering up after the storm quit."

"Fair enough."

"It's quiet out here. Peaceful. And it occurred to me that I've never really searched in this area. So, I set out. I stepped past the treeline, figuring that the shoulder back there would give me some kind of landmark to work with, and kept my eyes open. Three, four, five minutes on... I found it."

"What?"

Several moments passed and Elliott's pace quickened before he finally replied with a pointed finger. "*That,*" he announced, motioning into the distance.

The springy foliage and collected trunks all but chased out the sunlight. As such, the pair had to cover several more yards before Nicholas was able to make out the shape of the first tottering headstone. "What? What is that?"

Elliott, hands tucked into his pockets, gave a half shake of the head. "It's an old graveyard," he said quietly. "Long-forgotten. Long fallen into disrepair."

And so indeed it was. Sitting low in the swampy earth and scarfed in fetters of moss, grime, and age were several uneasy successions of grave markers. The monuments, left skewed and crooked by age, stretched deep into the wilderness ahead, and the inscriptions on most had been blurred by time. While the short path preceding this sight had not wanted for dampness of earth or coolness of air, the terrain of the forgotten cemetery possessed especial moisture, as well as that spine-tingling chilliness that is the product of shadow alone. A whiff or a glance left one without doubt; this was an ideal setting for fungi.

From the very first, as the duo began creeping through the morass and inserted themselves between sunken stones, mushrooms became apparent. The sodden landscape was littered with them. They sprang up in odd clusters, in varieties both clear-cut and rather dubious, from any surface that would have them—and, sometimes, even from those which ordinarily would not. Dewy crevasses in weathered headstones brought forth many-lobed hen-of-the-woods, and from the soupy lands themselves rebellious cordyceps struggled skyward. Trees all around were wreathed in turkey tail mushrooms of shocking hue. The blues and oranges left the strongest impressions in the gloom.

But these, though treasures in their own right, were glossed over without a word by Elliott as he trudged on. He stepped over heaps of handsome white buttons large enough to feed a family and made no remarks about the deposits of lion's manes whose long, white tendrils were truly worthy of the name. Instead, licking his lips repeatedly, he set his sights deeper in, to some secluded recess—one which he anticipated with a subtle lightening of complexion. "It isn't much further now," he promised.

The chef could not but marvel at the mushrooms on offer as they went. Any one of the edible species might have commanded a high price, for all on offer were uniform in their unique size and freshness. What's more, the proud colors the fungi bore, coupled with the hardiness of every stalk and cap in sight, promised exceptional nutrient density and unparalleled flavor. His mouth watered as he kept up with Elliott, so preoccupied was he by the culinary possibilities. *Those, there, would make an immaculate pasta filling. And these! Roasted, with garlic and oil—I could die a happy man. Ah, and what's this? The size of that shiitake puts any hamburger to shame!*

The stoop-shouldered peddler came to a halt so sudden that Nicholas scarcely avoided crashing into him. Clearing his throat, he slowly descended onto one knee and glanced at the chef over his shoulder, motioning to the ground. Just ahead, couched between two crooked grave markers, was a marshy declivity of perhaps two feet in depth where much rain had gathered. There was no standing water to be found there any longer; instead, the thirsty land had drunk it up, turning the divot into an utter mire of black soil and drowned foliage. It looked, in fact, almost as though one or both of the graves attested to by the aforementioned markers had been partially dug up. It was here, in this bed of rain-churned soil so very near to ancient bones, that the object of their search lay in wait. "Here they are," uttered Elliott.

Heedless of the grime, Nicholas joined Elliott on the ground and looked upon the sea of fungi before him. It was just as the man had reported; this shallow pit was filled to teeming with what appeared to be morel mushrooms. In keeping with the properties of all the aforeseen specimens, the morels in question were almost preternaturally robust. Black stalks terminated in the usual closed-umbrella-shaped tops, which were similarly black. Streaks of fiery crimson were laced throughout the caps, however, which in the low light seemed to glitter like red agate. This optical impression was perhaps furthered by the damp, for droplets of rain still clung to the porous mushroom-tops and reflected what little day-glow came worming down from the canopy.

Nicholas, whose training had been in Avignon, and who had sampled in his tenure most every edible mushroom common to cuisines both eastern and western, had never seen their like, and for several silent seconds he beheld them in awe. "They... they certainly do look like morels," he offered when his guide made no further comment.

"Yes, though I've never seen a morel with this coloration." Elliott leaned forward a bit, running his hands over the dewy pile. The entire growth, some feet high as well as across, was left trembling from his touch. "What do you think? Are they safe?"

At the merest pondering of their flavor, Nicholas's appetite was violently stirred. "They certainly *look* delicious..." He turned this way and that, studied the heap from a different angle, and admired their unique, fiery coloration. But it was then that he noticed something—something that saw him pause with a jerk.

Elliott, watching his companion closely for some moments, nodded weakly. "You've noticed, then?"

It had only come to him after taking in the mass of mushrooms as a whole and from a few different vantage points. The entire patch of curious morels was arranged in a most peculiar fashion—arranged, it so happened, in what he now realized was a recognizable schema. The totality of the newly discovered morel patch grew in the shape of a human being. The cluster's anthropoid outline was, after a series of shocked refusals, impossible to ignore, including a head and trunk. Segments representative of arms and legs had sufficient space from the bulk, leaving them clearly delineated. This was not all, however, for Nicholas's careful study of the soil brought something else to light—the crumbling, chalky substrate to which the morels clung for sustenance.

"Bones," gasped the chef, gaining his feet in a hurry. "T-Those are bones, aren't they?"

Elliott nodded slowly. "It would appear that one of these graves was disturbed by the elements, the body unearthed over time. The storm, it seems, finally brought it into the open."

"The storm only ended hours ago," snapped Nicholas. "How could all of these mushrooms have sprung from it in so little time?"

"Morels can spring up overnight," continued Elliott. "They don't need much time at all. It's interesting, though, the way they've taken to those bones. Look, here..." Still kneeling, he reached out and pointed to the nearest extremity—the segment answering for a head. Combing the hardy morels aside, he singled out what appeared to be a brittle human skull, both sockets clotted with sturdy tangles of mycelium. "Whatever these are, they're a true rarity indeed. *Corpse-fed...*" He dared a dark chuckle but soon returned to silence.

"So this is why you were acting so strangely earlier..."

"I didn't know what to make of it. I've never seen such a thing," confessed Elliott.

"It's disgusting."

"It's strange and upsetting. But it's also unique."

"Next, you're going to tell me that you know the poor sod..."

Elliott shook his head and reached out to the nearest gravestone. He slapped it with his palm. "Says here, *Giovanni Lopresti.*" He pointed at the other stone, slumping nearby. "That one says, *Thomas Pierre-Black.* In either case," he continued, motioning to the faded dates on the stones, "these guys have been dead since the turn of the last century. See? The first fellow passed on in 1901. His partner a few years later, in 1904. I've boasted of many things in my life, but I won't pretend that I was kicking around a hundred and twenty years ago. And you?"

The chef peered nauseously at the morels and took another glance at the bones beneath. "No... I suppose these bones *have* been here a long, long while. They've been worn down over time."

Elliott eased himself back onto his haunches and then sat down upon the wet ground. "The only question I have, Nicholas, is whether or not these are morels. What's your over-under?"

"They're morels," replied the chef. "I've never seen morels of this color, but... they're morels."

"So, we're in agreement, then?"

"Morels or not, I'd never serve such a thing. This is disgusting! The others we saw elsewhere—the button mushrooms, the cordyceps, sure. But this is grotesque. They're feeding off of human remains, Elliott. It's foul, it's—it's unethical!"

Elliott clicked his tongue and reached into the pit. With a careful tug, he loosed one of the morels, giving its stalk a hard pinch and inspecting it closely. He sniffed at the thing, patted the rain from its nooks and crannies. "Well, agree to disagree. If they're morels, they're safe to eat, no?"

"You aren't seriously going to try one, are you?"

"Do you think Giovanni will mind?"

"Uncooked? That's unwise."

"Tell you what," countered the mushroom peddler with a grin. "I'll taste-test them and let you know what I think. If I wind up in a bad way, you can drive me to the hospital."

"But Elliott!"

Giving the thing a final once-over, Elliott brought the morel to his mouth and bit off a portion of the cap. Conscious of the threat posed by poisonous or uncooked mushrooms, he was careful to eat only a small portion. "It's the dose that makes the poison, chef," he said while working it over in his mouth thoughtfully.

The words had no sooner left his mouth than he drew in a sharp breath, regarding the mushroom with wide eyes.

"What's the matter?" snapped Nicholas. "Is it offensive? Don't tell me you're about to drop dead..."

Elliott gave no reply whatsoever—except to suddenly stuff the remainder of the mushroom into his mouth. Cap, stalk, and all were milled ravenously between his teeth, and only a profusion of orgiastic moans kept him from swallowing it wholesale. These grunts of apparent pleasure grew so numerous and loud within him that breath began to fail him, and when he finally swallowed the thing, he did so with a gasp. Pawing at his mouth, he stared up at the canopy, panting.

"Elliott? Elliott!" nagged the chef, now with real concern. "Elliott?"

Out of nowhere, the mushroom peddler reached out and took Nicholas's hand in his, giving it a hard squeeze. When he turned to face the chef, it was with watery eyes. "It's... It's delicious," he whispered. His tongue danced across his lips as if in search of one last morsel. "I've never tasted anything like it..."

Nicholas drew his hand back. "You're being a bit melodramatic. Certain varieties of mushroom can be delicious without preparation, but most species require cooking to bring out their finest qualities."

"I've never tasted anything like it," insisted Elliott. "It's... It's incomparable. The flavor, the texture..." He was still panting, and his eyes strove hungrily toward the remaining fungi. "I need another taste. I need a bit more—"

"No, that'll be quite enough," spat the chef. "You're a braver man than I, eating one of those raw. For all we know there's toxin circulating through your system now, Elliott. Blood poisoning, liver failure—does that sound like a joke to you?"

Elliott donned a dreamy—and *earnest*—smile. "So be it. I'd throw it all away, and *more*, for another taste..."

Stunned at this admission, Nicholas paced around the heap of mushrooms with his hands in his pockets. "Don't be stupid, Elliott. It's just a mushroom. How good could it possibly taste? The morels of France—their flavor brings a smile to my face. But at the end of the day, a mushroom is a mushroom."

"Taste one for yourself and see."

"I'd rather not."

"I rather *would*," said Elliott, reaching out and plucking another. This time he didn't even pause to knock the rain from it, didn't even inspect it for insects or bits of detritus. The whole thing was promptly inhaled, and groans of unbelievable delight came pouring out of him.

"What if there's some hallucinogenic effect? I'm going to have to drag you back to the car at this rate."

Through tearful ecstasies, the mushroom peddler shook his head fervently. "My head is clear, Nicholas! My stomach, content. It's my taste that'll never be the same!" He reclined a little on the damp ground, as though the immensity of the flavor had bowled him over. "Simply incredible."

"What's so great about them?"

"I'd betray my own mother for the merest nibble."

"The flavors, Elliott! What has you so worked up?"

Though he lacked a culinary background, Elliott thoroughly detailed the flavor profile of this new discovery. "There is a pure, unrestrained savoriness about them," he began, while licking his chops. "It's sublime, greater than that of any other mushroom."

"The umami flavor, yes?"

"Yes, that's right. But that isn't all," continued Elliott. "On the back-end, there's a subtle but intoxicating sweetness. It lingers on the tongue and transitions beautifully from the initial savoriness. I've never experienced anything quite like it—not in a single foodstuff, at least. And the texture! There are some varieties I detest for their crunch or their rubberiness. Even raw, these almost melt in one's mouth. They're delicate, but not insubstantial. Am I making sense? From the mouth-feel, down to the flavor, they're utterly perfect."

This rave review more than piqued the young chef's curiosity—so much so that he began to overlook the morbid bed in which they lay. "They're better than your usual morels, then?" he asked.

"They aren't even in the same league. Those others? The hogs can have at them!"

The fresh, local morels that Elliott had been in the habit of bringing to La Brasserie had ranked among the best that Nicholas had ever tasted. To hear that these mysterious new fungi trumped them on every front was an exciting enough prospect to blunt his judgment. "And you say you don't feel ill?"

"Not yet, anyway," replied Elliott. "I won't lie to you, chef, raw mushrooms are always a gamble. But these... oh, I feel *more* than good. With the wickeder lots, you often know it straight away. With these? Well, I wouldn't be surprised if they held some salutary effect or another. I feel invigorated!"

"You don't say..."

"I don't know what these are, Nicholas. I don't know if they're a new discovery. Perhaps they are. Whatever the case, we must harvest them. We must take as many as we can carry. And on Monday, you must serve them!" He motioned to the pit and lovingly stroked the tops of the mushrooms. "Here is your Michelin star!"

Convinced by his partner, Nicholas knelt down once more. "All right, then. Let's gather them. Take as many as you can. Promise me, though, that you'll never tell anyone about where we found them, Elliott."

"I would never!" declared the mushroom hawker.

"It would cause a scandal if people found out that I was drawing mushrooms from such an... *unconventional* place..."

"Corpse-fed, you mean?" replied Elliott with a laugh. He began ripping up mushrooms and funneling them into his pockets. "Oh, once people get a taste of these, I don't think they'll care where they came from. The only thing they'll be worried about is their next bite!"

"Sure, but promise me, Elliott."

"Yes, yes, I promise." He lifted his cap as if preparing to stuff away a secret. "I'll keep it under my hat."

Together, the pair carried off the whole mess of morels. Hauling them in their upturned shirts, they hobbled back to the car, where they poured them out into the trunk. The emptying of the pit required a few trips, and by the last the sun was in full retreat and the woods were bathed in misty gloom. This dimming proved a small mercy, for it prevented both men from getting a very clear look at the human remains from which their quarry had sprung.

Filthy now, the duo took their seats in the sedan and made a hard turn back onto the road. Headlights engaged, they flew swiftly from the remote shoulder and planned to head straight for Nicholas's home. There, the chef intended to experiment with these new mushrooms.

While passing back into town, Elliott went clawing through his pocket and unearthed a single straggler—a black and red morel of medium size. Hands shaking with excitement, he prepared to bring it to his lips, but the chef stopped him short, asking, "Say, let me have a taste, will you?"

"What?" The greedy passenger looked as though he'd just been slapped across the face.

"Just a taste. I want to see if they're really as good as you say."

"Ah, but it *is* rather unsafe," offered Elliott.

"Don't be that way! Just give me a nibble, will you?" He held out his hand in anticipation.

Elliott acquiesced with a noxious smile. "O-Of course... I'd love to hear your thoughts..." He placed the morel in Nicholas's palm and watched closely as the chef took a small bite of the cap.

At once, the flavor proved almost overwhelming. Nicholas was overcome by a tidal wave of savoriness so profound that he half felt himself in a dream. Tires screeched as he pulled onto the side of the road and slammed the brakes, bringing them to a stop. His bite, initially curious and exploratory, grew ravenous as his mouth became better acquainted with the stuff, and he chewed up the piece of mushroom cap with the vigor of a starved man at a banquet. His ears and neck tingled with pleasure and his mouth watered like a fountain. And then, just as quickly, the promised sweetness came rushing in and left his tongue buzzing with the gentleness of raw honey.

It was no mere food that he had eaten; the thing he'd just put into his mouth had been a full-on sensory experience. He was filled to the brim with excitement and didn't even hear the delighted sounds issuing from his lips until Elliott's laughter broke in and made him once again aware of himself.

"See? They *are* good, aren't they?"

The chef struggled to regain his breath. His tongue ran circuits around the inside of his mouth, chasing down the last hints of that superspectral flavor. "*Good* isn't a strong enough word..."

"Divine! Not of this world!"

"Superb."

When next he wheeled onto the road, he mashed the accelerator in a frenzy. The path to his home was blazed at speeds greater than the posted limits and with no regard for traffic lights.

With muddy hands, the pair stood in the kitchen, staring at their bounty heaped upon the countertop. They hadn't counted, but instinct told them that they'd gathered up somewhere between 100 and 150 mushrooms. The things seeped old rain from every crevice and filled the small room with an earthy scent.

Dinner plans were drawn up at once. As the chef rummaged excitedly through his cabinets and spoke much of braises and complementary herbs, Elliott hovered by the counter and adored the things. Nicholas popped a sensible vintage from his personal stores and poured two generous glasses while arranging bottles of oil and other ingredients by the stove.

In time, though, as the wine went untouched and the other ingredients came to room temperature, it became clear that both men had become preoccupied by other designs.

"You'll hate me for saying it," put forth Elliott, who'd been perched uneasily on a kitchen stool for some minutes. He'd been swirling his wine glass mechanically, making pretensions toward aeration, but now wished to make it clear that he was reserving his palate for other, greater pleasures. "Must we cook them?" For fear that the chef might complain, he hurriedly continued, "It's just that they're so delicious as they are! The texture may not hold up against high temperatures, and..."

Nicholas, having been on a similar mental track, nodded. "It's a good question. What could I add to them? How can I improve upon what nature has done?" He toyed with the skillet in his hand and then set it upon the stove with a sigh. "Incorporating them in a salad, perhaps, would be the best way."

"A salad! Yes! Fresh and raw, they'll be the star of the show."

"Provided, of course, that they're safe."

"Oh, but they are, chef. They are!" Elliott took to his feet and snatched a morel off the counter cavalierly. "We'd both be dead by now if these were poisonous, I'm sure." Unable to override his desire, he stuffed the thing into his mouth and went weak in the knees. "Yes, oh, *yes*, they're safe! And they mustn't be cooked, chef. They mustn't be!"

Nicholas, availing himself of another morel, made a great show of inspecting it. He worked his fingertip across the cap, searching beneath its frills for signs of filth or disease. He, too, scarfed down his mushroom, and the surge of flavor that ensued was enough to make his heart race. "They *do* seem quite safe, don't they?"

"Safe as sugar! Safe as table salt, chef!" spat Elliott, helping himself to yet another.

"Perhaps," panted Nicholas, eyeing the mound longingly, "we should send a few to a lab. A trained mycologist will be able to test them and tell us precisely what they are. Then we'd know if it's a new species..."

"What a waste!" cried the ruddy glutton, cheeks packed with succulent stalks. "No, no! Let us enjoy ourselves, chef. Let us enjoy our discovery. We will hold back a certain amount for the dinner service on Monday, yes?"

"And the rest," replied the chef, "we can keep for ourselves."

"That's right!"

"It's only sensible that a cook should have strong acquaintance with his ingredients," said Nicholas. "I've tasted but a few. There may be other dimensions to these mushrooms..." He snatched up another—larger, this time—and bit into its damp flesh as though it were a banana. Waves of pleasure saw him sink against the edge of the counter as he gulped the morel down. His every taste bud quaked in awe of the native savoriness, nearly to the point of soreness, only to be soothed by the Dionysian sweetness that always followed.

The specimen he'd availed himself of was the largest one he'd yet tried, a mushroom necessitating at least three or four bites. He had not made a very careful examination of the morel in question until the moment when he reared back in preparation for his second bite. It was then that he noticed, in one of the dark crannies of the cap, an insect was stirring. Some many-legged thing, black in color and beetle-like, buzzed fearfully in the mushroom. Such things were not unexpected; freshly picked, unwashed produce almost always contained these hangers-on. Nicholas had never been great at dealing with bugs and would ordinarily have been too disgusted at the sight of the thing to continue snacking.

Somehow, though, his disgust was absent. In fact, as he watched the little beetle strain and scurry within the cap, he felt nothing save a desire to proceed. He could not bring himself to evict the thing, nor to rinse the mushroom off. He could not bring himself to do *anything* that might possibly delay his enjoyment any longer. Without giving the matter any further thought, he crammed the rest of the morel into his mouth and began to chew. The deluge of flavor recommenced. The thing's intoxicating texture was briefly interrupted by the graininess of some twitching addition, but whatever it was that came seeping from that ruptured thorax, or whatever the bitterness of its chitinous legs, the taste of the beetle failed to lower his enjoyment one iota.

Elliott, leaning against the counter as if for dear life, was beginning to push handfuls of the morels into his mouth. He sucked them down faster than he could chew them, and when the slurry of half-masticated mushrooms and thick spittle came running down his chin and neck, he studiously cupped it back up in his hands and drank it down like a soup.

Between bites, when breath allowed, both men hooted and hollered like none since the fall of Rome. Mere intemperance gave way to vaster gluttonies, and before long the two were on their knees, greedily knocking armfuls of the morels onto the linoleum that they might squat down and devour them like dogs.

Thus went the pile of mysterious mushrooms. When all was said and done and both men had lost consciousness in the kitchen, reeling in flavorful ecstasies, not so much as a crumb remained. Each of them took turns licking down the countertops, ensuring that not even a drop of the mushroom-flavored water would go to waste.

Sleep came while they stroked at their bulging bellies, weeping and splayed on the floor.

***

When Nicholas awoke, he was alone.

Scraping his sweat-slick bulk off the floor, he went hobbling toward the stove. The clock readout told him he'd been asleep several hours; the world was on the verge of dawn. "Elliott?" he called out, blurry eyes combing the dark corners in search of the mushroom peddler. He was nowhere to be found, however. *Probably slipped out before I woke up,* he thought to himself.

The chef had awakened in quite a state. His sleep had been a feverish one; after binging on the mysterious morels, he and Elliott both had essentially collapsed, and beyond that point, Nicholas could only remember being plagued by a terrible inner heat. His dreams—if the fragmented, unhappy visions he'd suffered could even be called dreams—had been chaotic.

He went limping through the house and appraised himself in the bathroom mirror after taking several handfuls of water to the face and neck. Nothing much seemed wrong; though he looked like a man who'd spent an uncomfortable night sleeping on the kitchen floor, his complexion proved normal and his eyes and tongue sported no irregularities. It was possible that the morels had carried with them a slight hallucinogenic effect—at least, when eaten in great quantities—but they hadn't left him with any notable problems.

The delicious mushrooms, then, were safe.

They were also gone.

Unable to control their appetites, Elliott and Nicholas had gorged on the things, leaving none for him to serve his customers on Monday evening. It was regrettable, but as he paced through the house and regained his bearings, he laughed a little and put it out of his mind. He'd had many strange and interesting culinary experiences all over the world—experiences that he could not hope to reproduce. This, he felt, had simply been another. Perhaps he and Elliott would be able to rummage up more of the black and red morels in the future. Until then, he would content himself by serving his usual fare.

Sunday morning came and went, and by afternoon the young chef found himself faced with a strange problem. Habit had seen him prepare a pot of coffee and a light breakfast, but both went cold before he could summon up his appetite. The spread simply held no allure, and though he told himself it was important to eat, he never once brought a mug or fork to his lips. It was out of character; on his rare days off, he quite liked to treat himself to sumptuous meals and snacks. "I must have really packed it in last night," he told himself while clearing the mess away.

Thinking that the binge of the night previous had left him stuffed or somehow impacted his digestion, he changed clothes and went for a light jog around the neighborhood—though this was very short-lived on account of a sudden soreness in the knees and ankles. He returned to his home an achy wreck and applied ice to the joints in question until the pain ebbed. Even so, his appetite did not deign to reappear.

By that evening, he hadn't eaten in more than eighteen hours. Where usually such a fast would have been met with lightheadedness and frustration, Nicholas was instead calm and composed—and not at all hungry. He thought it most strange, though in light of the huge bolus of calories he'd consumed with Elliott, he waved off alarm. As the sun set, he fixed himself a light meal of scrambled eggs made with crème fraîche and a side of scalloped potatoes—a comfortable favorite of his.

Sitting at the kitchen table with a bit of Rachmaninoff on the stereo, he realized with horror that he could not bear to eat the meal that he had so carefully prepared and had eaten with relish in the past. He approached the eggs and potatoes a number of times, but in bringing forkfuls to his lips was filled to bursting with disgust. The food had not merely lost its appeal; compared to the incredible morels he'd eaten with Elliott, the eggs and potatoes did not strike him as food. Yes, that was the source of his troubles. His heart and stomach were in agreement. They wanted one thing, and one thing only: more of the black and red morels. Nothing else would do.

Throwing away his dinner, he made do with a bit of mineral water and tried to placate himself with other entertainments. A baseball game on TV, an action movie, a bout of scrolling on social media—none of these could hold him for very long. The more he tried to distance himself from the delectable morels, the more he fixated on them.

"Nothing can be done. They're all gone." He and Elliott had collected every one of the mushrooms from the gravesite. It was possible that more had turned up overnight, but he thought it mighty unlikely.

But then, it was not *so* unlikely. "Morels can spring up overnight, can't they? At least, that's what Elliott claimed," he uttered to himself. "Perhaps there *are* more waiting for me there."

And this time, venturing alone into the woods, he would be able to harvest them all for *himself*.

Stepping out of the car and onto the damp shoulder, Nicholas was surprised to find the soreness in his joints had not abated. It was getting worse, as though the cartilage in each had grown sparse, leading to the friction of bone on bone. He struggled to the tree-line, wincing and stretching, and tried to remember the exact route he'd taken the evening previous. There was a bit of sun left in the sky, and by this glow, which seeped through the treetops, he quickly found himself in the presence of several ancient headstones.

Once more, he was greeted by mounds of robust mushrooms, but these he passed without a second glance as he searched for the open grave. The turkey tails, the white buttons—these meant nothing to him. Somewhere in this wilderness—just a little further ahead, he kept telling himself—he would find the site. Perhaps he would find an eruption of the elusive morels, a fresh bounty rivaling that of the day before. Maybe he would find only a smattering. In either case, he intended to claim what he could and get his fill. Gone were fantasies of serving the mushrooms to paying customers. Weighed against the flavor of these new fungi, his Michelin ambitions were null.

Though less wet than the previous day, the terrain remained somewhat slick and muddy, leading to ill footing and a few trip-ups as he stepped between the ancient graves. He went clopping from one muddy trench to another, his sneakers unfit for the task, and was almost stripped of his footwear on a number of occasions by the sucking mire. It was for this reason that he lost his balance and fell—and, in falling, earned a startling injury.

Nicholas tumbled to his right as though a rug had been pulled out from under his feet, and throwing out his arms in search of support he found a stubborn old tombstone. This, his right forearm met with a sickening crack before he went rolling onto the ground with a moan. Searing pain coursed through him as he felt the skin of his arm parted by splintered bone; he knew, before he could even sit upright and glance at the injury, that the fracture had come bursting through the surface.

Blood and bone and connective tissue should have awaited him as he turned a wide eye to the arm in question. Instead, as he surveyed the injury, which had erupted very near the elbow, he found nothing of the sort. The skin had been pierced, yes, by a single splinter of white, bloodless bone, but there was not so much as a drop of gore to be found. Instead, where blood and muscle should've reared their heads, coarse filaments, black and red in color, spilled out in tangled threads. These thin cords, evidently wrapped tightly around the bones of his forearm, pulsed subtly as he beheld them in terror—pulsed like veins or arteries.

But they were not veins or arteries—at least, not in the human sense.

Struggling onto his knees, Nicholas teased the exposed cordage with his fingers. It felt vaguely rubbery; tough, like wire, but undoubtedly organic.

The threads wound around his bones felt like *roots*.

Aghast, the chef clutched at his wounded arm and gained his feet. Standing proved more difficult than ever before as his knees popped and whined for the effort. Were his leg bones, his other joints, also tangled in these mycelium-like threads?

No! he told himself. *You're hallucinating. You must've hit your head on the way down. You're fine. You're going to be all right. You just need to get to a doctor. Take a deep breath and relax...*

Suddenly unsure of his bearings, Nicholas shuffled a little from the tombstone that'd split his arm and went looking for the unconventional path he'd cut through the wilderness.

Instead, a stone's throw to his left, he discovered what appeared to be a shallow grave, lately disturbed.

And in it, something *writhing*.

Nicholas staggered toward the open grave, his sneakers squelching in the mud. The scene came gradually into focus: the rain-softened borders of the site, the duo of crooked stones that framed it, the man-sized thing that flopped and groaned and whined within its shallow depths.

The one in the grave was none other than Elliott. Hatless, jacket-less Elliott was floundering in the declivity, face-down. His face and arms were black with soil and his legs kicked feebly, as if he were trying to bend his knees and arise. It soon became apparent that he could not, and that these were the stirrings of a creature in its death throes.

"Elliott?" gasped the chef, rushing over as quickly as his feet could take him. "Elliott? What's happened?"

The mushroom peddler jerked at the sound of Nicholas's voice and with a monumental effort turned his head to try and meet him. The gesture came with a series of cries and moans, as though the slightest pivot of the head could not be executed without unbelievable pain. "N-Nicholas..." he sighed, his black lips parting and his tongue thudding noisily within his dry mouth. "So... you've come too..."

The chef clutched at his arm and drew nearer the grave. "Elliott, what's happened to you? What's—" Surveying the prone man, Nicholas happened upon something that'd earlier eluded him—a terrible injury, previously hidden by the hem of Elliott's blackened slacks. The man's ankle was split open and his foot had been bent hideously inward in a devastating breakage. The injury itself, though, was not half as terrible as the thing which had come creeping out of the ruptured foot.

A small morel, black and red, had sprung defiantly out of Elliott's broken ankle. Twitching threads peeked out of the bloodless, fleshy fissure as they drew sustenance from the bones and tissues within him.

"I had to have more..." wheezed the mushroom peddler. "And so... I left. I left your place, Nicholas. And I returned here." He clutched at the old bones beneath him as he went on. "There were no more morels. Not even one! But that didn't stop me, Nicholas. No. I ate as much of this soil as I could bear in the hopes of finding just *one more scrap.* I sucked on these weathered bones, ripped the roots off them with my teeth... but found only bitterness.

"The morels we so enjoyed... they're not gone. They're living within us now, Nicholas. Within us! I collapsed here after I hurt my foot. I don't... I don't feel well. The stiffness in my joints... and the coolness..." He gave a withered laugh. "I feel half-dead already. The morels... they're spread throughout my body and they're sucking everything out of me. And soon... all too soon... I'll be sleeping in this grave just like the poor sap we first found here. We're doomed, Nicholas. We're doomed. We should not have eaten the things. We shouldn't have disturbed the dead! And yet... and yet I *still* long for a taste! How cruel it is, to meet one's end this way... to pass from this life without one... more... taste..."

Nicholas listened to the man as he wept in the pit. No tears came from Elliott's eyes; the water and nutrients essential to tears had already been committed to other processes by the ever-pulsing threads of mycelium. Glancing at his wounded arm, he thought he spied the cap of a morel forming deep within the damaged tissues. He felt a great pressure behind his eyes as he stared, as though morels might spring out of his brain and send his eyeballs tumbling out of their sockets. His mouth was dry and, conscious now of what was happening to him, he felt woozy.

"We should not have eaten them," mourned Elliott in the grave. "There is nothing to be done for us, Nicholas."

"No cure."

"It's too late. I haven't got the strength to stand, to walk…"

"It's already in me," replied Nicholas. "My arm… my head… I'm full of them."

"Would that I could taste them one last time," sobbed the mushroom peddler.

Nicholas lowered himself to the ground and leaned into the open grave where Elliott twitched. "Nothing can be done," he said, eyeing the morel that jutted from the man's broken ankle. "Nothing at all. So… what good will it do to deprive one's self?" He licked his lips and scurried a little deeper in, approaching Elliott's foot. "What's one last taste, between friends?"

Pinning Elliott's leg down with his good arm, the chef homed in on the morel and tore it away with sharp teeth. His bite brought with it more than the mushroom; he took with him no little flesh and was greeted by Elliott's sharp scream as he feasted. The man's tissues were bloodless, flavorless—almost gummy in texture, having been robbed of all vitality.

But Elliott's flesh could not detract from his enjoyment of the morel.

Chewing through mushroom, sinew, and skin, the young chef was overwhelmed by the profound savoriness in whose wake the gentle sweetness always came.

The sweetness did arrive.

And it never ended.

He died with the perfect sweetness on his tongue, having savored it ecstatically until tear ducts and taste buds alike had grown heavy with new morels.

The Smell of Old Paper

I CAN'T RECALL, NOW, what it was that brought me into the attic on that cool spring afternoon.

It'd been raining all day, and my house, you must understand, has never done particularly well during the soggier seasons. Its corners and closets are given to mold, prone to blackish-green outbreaks. Perhaps it was something related to this—a casual investigation of some leak or moldy odor—that saw me venture into the attic.

Once, I'd considered turning the attic into a study or library of some sort—a retreat where I could house my vast collection of books and perhaps play at writing my own. The space had proven a bad fit for such activities, though, what with its tendency toward dizzying heat in the summer and bone-chilling cold in the winter, and I quickly abandoned my plans, using it instead as a storage space.

Holiday decorations in crumpled cardboard boxes were ferried to and fro each year until I gradually lost my taste for decorating and left them stranded in heaps. What few things I'd inherited from my late mother were also stored in the attic—a few sentimental odds and ends in plastic crates. Never having been able to throw away a perfectly good book, I'd collected many dog-eared volumes there, too—books that I was unlikely to revisit, but that I couldn't bear to part with.

On that spring afternoon the cramped attic was alive with a striking contrast of dewy light and dusty shadow. Met with the unsightly piles, the utter mess, I began to consider a culling. I pawed at this or that accretion, wondering, as a stranger might, just what each box and bag contained. Surely, I didn't need to keep *all* of these things; some would make worthy donations, while others were simply taking up space and, probably, worsening my home's romance with mold.

I rummaged through boxes of well-loved books, rediscovering volumes that I had once fawned over. My notes remained in their margins, their covers were marred with splotches of spilled tea and coffee, and the spines of many were half-broken, telling of numerous late-night rereadings. By the light that stole in through the single circular window, I stumbled headlong into the world of the past, reading bits of fiction and philosophy under my breath and delightedly grasping at the robes of my long-spent youth.

Time has a way of flattening one's youth and its attendant naivete. It steamrolls strength and quiets ambition, too. Outwardly, the young man and the old appear almost different species, despite housing the same yearnings. I flipped through the marginalia, amused, embarrassed, and still rooting for the dilettante who'd penned it all so many moons prior, and might have *really* enjoyed my trip down memory lane if not for what happened next.

The note had been lying in wait for years. It slipped out of the book I held, landing upon the floor with a faint rustle. A single page of yellowed paper, folded; a stowaway pressed between the chapters of a beaten hardback. It was creased throughout, having undergone many readings and refoldings, and had grown so thin at the bend that the edges felt feather-like between my fingers.

More than the book it had been hiding in, more than the mounds of mementos that surrounded me in the dusty attic, the letter exuded a particular smell: the smell unique to old paper. It has been said that, of all the senses, smell is the one most linked to memory. It must be so, because no sooner did I catch a whiff of the page than I realized with a shocking suddenness just what it was—and, with a somersault of the heart, who had written it.

And when I remembered, I almost didn't bother to read it. Almost.

I *did*, eventually, work up the gumption to unfold it, sitting cross-legged on the attic floor. Many, many years had passed since my last glance, but as I started into it, I found the opening line still etched into my memory.

So, I guess this is goodbye, Michael.

The only woman I've ever really loved died at twenty-two.

We never fought, Allegra and I. Four years of dating and I can't recall a heated argument, a single shouting match. We'd fallen in together as college freshmen after getting paired in a few lectures, and soon took to chasing one another around campus. Neither of us had ever been in a serious relationship before, and the attachment that grew up between us probably seemed unhealthy to our peers. We spent all of our free time together; an effortless expenditure, really, because we thrived on each other's company. Somehow, I felt as though I'd always known her, and she claimed to feel the same.

Dating for such a length of time, it was only natural that conversations about the future should take place, and in the future I imagined for myself I had erected a place for her. The topic of marriage had been thrown around enough that, one assumed, we were both slow-walking toward the altar.

Allegra, though, had other plans.

An ambitious student, she'd been offered a handful of exciting opportunities at schools across the country—schools that could open doors for her in the future, but that would take her far from the life I'd intended to build for us. I'd just completed my degree, and had lined up a decent job right out of school. The time was fast approaching for me to shop around for a new place, and maybe a ring.

I never got that far, though.

Forced to decide between a future with me in our little college town and an admittedly prestigious opportunity at her dream university, Allegra chose the latter. During our last few meetups, as work kept me increasingly busy, she struck me by turns as melancholy and uncomfortable, and I realize now that it's because she was grappling with her decision.

She eventually made her choice, and I only found out about it on account of the handwritten letter she dropped into my apartment's mail slot. Allegra didn't call, didn't arrange a final face-to-face meeting, but instead shot off a brief note informing me that I'd lost the race. It was worded prettily enough, of course—even in this last gesture she'd been sweet enough to dismiss me in glowing terms, and to hint, however pointlessly, at some future reunion.

I knew it was over. She was on her way to Palo Alto to begin a new life. She'd certainly meet a new guy at this new school, and the future I'd envisioned for us both would play out beautiful-ly—except that my role would be played by someone else. I had no delusions about a future rekindling of our romance, about making nice down the line and picking up where we'd left off. The letter hit me like a truck, and for days after receiving it I was overcome by numbness.

The letter, technically, marked the end of things between us, but it wasn't the last I heard from Allegra. She reached out to me a final time, about two weeks after heading west. Neck-deep in work and bitter at how things had ended, I didn't bother picking up the phone the night she called, instead letting it go to voicemail. Three times her number flashed across my phone screen, and three times I ignored it. I didn't bother listening to her message until a few days later, when my curiosity got the better of me.

The calls had come rather late, and in her message I could hear the hum of an engine in the background. *"Michael, it's me. I'm sorry about everything. Can you please pick up? I need to talk to you. I... I've had second thoughts. This degree program... I've been thinking about it, but it isn't what I really want. I'm heading back home. I know it's late, but I'll be in town in the next few hours if you want to meet up. I'm sorry, Michael..."*

I was troubled by the voicemail—not the least because days had passed since Allegra had left it, and she'd never turned up at my door or tried to call again. After listening to it, I wrestled with my pride for a few hours before finally dialing her with a mind toward venting my spleen. I wasn't sure I was willing to take her back after she'd ended things so callously. The idea of patching things up and continuing as normal seemed impossible to me in that moment. I was hurt. I was angry. I was feeling more than a little resentful.

And so, imagine my surprise when her mother answered the phone after a few rings.

Allegra's folks had always been kind. I'd met them numerous times over the years, and sensing their daughter's happiness, they'd been supportive of our relationship. Whatever my mood at the time of the call, I couldn't find it in myself to be rude to her mother, and all the vitriol I'd been brewing suddenly receded. My anger shrank all the more when the woman's threadbare *Hello?* came through the receiver and it first occurred to me that something might be wrong.

A lot had happened since that voicemail had been left, apparently.

When asked what, exactly, had made Allegra lose control of her car and sent it barreling full-speed into a concrete barrier, none could say. A spot of rain, which had made the roads slick, was put forth as one potential culprit. Fog rolling across a rural stretch of highway was another. But these, even if accessories to the fatal accident, could not be charged. None were present at the time of the crash; it was called in some time after the fact by a passing semi-driver. The vehicle itself had been totaled, and the driver, all were assured in the interest of maximizing consolation, had died on impact, sans prolonged suffering.

The sufferings she'd been spared, one could say, had been inherited by the rest of us.

My instinct was to crumple the note, to burn it, to do whatever necessary to part myself from the painful memory the thing had roused, but in the end I refolded it and tucked it once again into the hardcover that had been its home for so many years. Having lost my taste for nostalgia, I no longer had any urge to rummage and I wasn't long in leaving the attic altogether, slamming the pull-down door violently as I went.

There is nothing more to tell of the story that cannot be inferred from what I have already shared. I never married because I could never make room in my heart for anyone the way I'd done for Allegra. I threw myself into work in my mourning, as so many are prone to do, and kept on until I could afford a comfortable—if unexciting—life. Most of the time, I am a stranger to the unpleasant past of which that yellowed note is an aching reminder. I do not think of such things often, and when they do rear their heads I have become quite skilled at letting them fizzle out before they can threaten my mood.

But having come into contact with the note again after so many years—having touched, as it were, an *artifact* of that other world and all its loss, I felt myself defiled and haunted by the past. I remember that I showered that afternoon after I came down from the attic. I told myself that it was on account of the dust and potential mold, when in truth I only showered in the hopes that I might scrub my feelings away. The day, if you can pardon me for sounding melodramatic, was ruined by the reopening of old wounds, and I passed my time pacing the quiet rooms of my home. The memories I'd become so adept at dodging had gained the upper hand; I could no longer oust them. I had no choice but to bear them patiently.

And then the night came.

The day's rain worsened and brought with it rumblings of distant thunder. The winds beat upon the house and all but uprooted the trees outside my windows. Thinking it perfect weather for a deep doze, I ate only a meager dinner and prepared myself for an early bedtime, trading my usual reading or television for a cup of hot herbal tea. I made it only halfway through the mug when sleep came for me, and I let myself go freely, eager to awaken to a clean mental slate.

But sleep remained at my bedside for only a short while; not long past midnight, it left its post and wakefulness stole in. I awoke to a scene of relative peace, for the storm had petered out and, except for the odd drippings on the roof and the fainter lashings of a dying wind, the world was silent as a sepulcher.

The *outside* world, that is.

My chief reason for awakening at all was that some noise—amplified by the silence without—had caught my notice. Fished from the deep waters of a restful sleep, I thrashed a little in my bed and tried, half-cognizantly, to reconnect with the bothersome sound that'd awakened me.

Though I sat up for some minutes, blinking in the darkness, I heard nothing. The walls of my room were waxy with shadow, leaving my tired eyes to trace fantastical shapes into the ether when my ears could not pin down the mysterious source of noise. This lengthy wait seemed to indicate that there hadn't been a noise—that I'd come to by mere chance, and would soon plummet back into restfulness if only I could stop listening to the dark.

Sleep wedged its foot in the door of my mind and seemed on the verge of walking back in when, suddenly, I heard something. This time, more or less possessed of my faculties, I could in no way deny that my sense of hearing had been tripped. But... by *what?* What could be the source, the meaning, of such a strange noise in the dead of night? I have no pets to blame such disturbances on, no housemates to point fingers at. My thoughts immediately turned to creeping intruders—though the nature of the sound hardly lent itself to the realities of home invasion.

I can only describe what I heard as a faint rustling.

One who has heard the noise of dead leaves skittering across pavement in late autumn knows something of the sound I heard that night; but then, perhaps its *nearest* equivalent is the crumpling of thin paper. It came from somewhere beyond my bedroom door, emanated from the inky sliver of hallway which was just barely perceptible from where I sat. Sure now of what I was hearing, I stood up and prepared to investigate, breath locked tightly within my chest.

I approached the door like a thief and wrapped my fingers gingerly around its uppermost edge; then, by small degrees, I opened it and—when I had made space enough to comfortably step into the hall—at once swiped at the light switch on the wall. It had been my intention to sneak up on the thing responsible for this noise—a mouse or other small pest, I had begun to suspect. Instead, when the lights flashed on and my tired eyes had had a chance to grapple with the new brightness, I found there was nothing to see.

But there *was*, it turned out, much to *smell.* Where my eyes and ears failed to pick up the culprit's trail, my nose was visited by the reek of old paper. The scent was intense, bringing to mind a moldering library, and it hung so thickly in the air that I couldn't keep from coughing as I stood there, stupefied. Nevertheless, I found nothing in the hall; the sound and odor both seemed utterly rootless. Shambling forward a few steps and pawing the veil of sleep from my eyes, I turned the corner and visited the living room. Shortly thereafter, I made a contemplative tour of the kitchen. The smell dissipated and the sound made no reprise.

Until, that is, I found myself approaching the stumpy segment of hall whose ceiling is home to the attic door. The scent of old paper was strengthened there, and from up above I heard another bout of the tell-tale rustling. More alarming, however, was the sight of the attic pull-down door sitting open, with the rickety wooden ladder fully extended. I knew that I had slammed the thing shut that afternoon and that I hadn't returned to it since—and I knew in that instant, too, the sound that had awakened me.

It'd been the sound of the attic door being thrown forcefully open.

But by whom?

The thing required no little force to operate; whether opening it from above or below, undoing the latch took a good bit of effort. On account of its design, it could not simply have fallen open, perfectly extending its attached ladder like a stuck-out tongue. No, *someone* had opened it while I was asleep in the other room and, in descending, had brought with them the powerful odor of old paper. The faint rustle of their approach and the shedding of that antique musk had filled the hall outside my room—but by the time I'd gathered the courage and wherewithal to investigate, the individual had staged a retreat.

And now, as a furtive rustling issued from the black rectangle above me, I had found them.

Shuddering, I dug my heels into the carpet and summoned up what bark I could. "Who goes there?" I bellowed. "I know you're up there. Show yourself, and don't make any sudden moves!"

No sooner was the command shouted did I regret my voicing of it, however.

From the nighted rectangle in the ceiling there emerged a thin, white arm. Half-limp, almost boneless, the limb strove toward the topmost rung of the ladder, whereupon five pale fingers dug tremblingly into the wood. From this same expanse there came a second arm, repeating the maneuvers of the first—and all this in service of dragging a lank, bloodless torso out into the open. Tangles of brown, wavy hair drooped vine-like across the ceiling as the figure slipped out on its belly, like a serpent. Writhing spasmodically, the slender form—a pasty human corpse studded with bluish vessels as readable as routes on a road atlas—jerked and slithered between the rungs, making a gradual descent into the hallway.

And all the while, there came the rustling. *The damnable rustling*. It wasn't a product of the thing's strange movements or even the sound of its dragging its cold flesh against wood or carpet. No, it was the thing's *voice*. It spoke the language of crumpled paper, of windswept leaves; the language of old books and older memories left to molder.

I knew that it was Allegra. No matter how tousled, I recognized her hair. I recognized her milk-white hands and the rings on her fingers as they sometimes *clacked* against the rungs. I even recognized the clothes she was wearing—the ratty jeans and gray university sweatshirt, both streaked in green and black mold. But the thing crawling out of the attic toward me, the thing that had answered my call, and which filled the air with the necrotic perfume of forgotten books, lacked one thing.

A face.

Beneath the knots of brown hair, I could not discern Allegra's face. Instead, where that beautiful countenance had once been, I saw only a creased and weathered surface, vaguely face-like in shape, but boasting no human features. Where her face had once been there was only crumpled paper now. *That* was where the constant rustling was coming from. The creases, the wrinkles on the featureless veil were alive; they danced and shrank and multiplied across the yellowed surface in numberless varieties of voiceless expression. The crumpled paper mask contorted forcefully as Allegra strained to communicate, but only the rustling won out—the sound, perhaps, of yearnings, of important things left unsaid.

The figure met the carpet with a flop and then shuffled toward me on hands and knees, the rustling reaching a maddening crescendo. I was stung by fear and disgust as I stood there, and for some dread moments I backed away from her, until I was against the wall and I could retreat no further. Still she proceeded, and as she groped pitifully through the dark house after me, I found myself filled, too, with grief.

"Allegra?" I chanced.

Only then did the figure pause. Only then, when I'd addressed her by her name, did the rustling cease.

"Allegra," I continued. "I'm sorry. I'm sorry I didn't pick up the phone that night."

The figure looked upward, meeting me with her crumpled visage.

"You called that night to apologize, to try and work things out, but I ignored you." I took a step toward her. "I should have answered, but I was too upset. *I'm* the one who should be sorry, Allegra." I dared another step. "Anyway, I forgive you. If you had shown up at my place that night, I would have taken you back. Of course I would've. You're the only woman I've ever loved. Decades have passed and that hasn't changed."

I felt a tightening in my chest, the ache of incoming tears as I started toward her in earnest. "Allegra—" I said, wiping at my eyes.

No sooner did I wipe my tears and stumble a few paces down the hall did the figure vanish. I came to a sudden halt, finding myself alone in the hallway, standing before an open attic door. I kneaded at my eyes again and panned around the hall, the adjacent rooms, the attic above, but found no sign of her except the lingering smell of old paper.

"Allegra? Are you... Are you still here?"

There was no reply. The rustling had ceased once and for all.

I've since sold off all of my old books. Holding onto the past, to nostalgic bits and bobs, no longer strikes me as healthy. I dropped off the whole trunkload at a local secondhand shop, and managed to pare down the contents of my attic to just a few select boxes. With the books gone, I find I can breathe easier—and it may just be my imagination, but since parting with my clutter I believe that the house is no longer as damp. Anyhow, I've noticed much less mold, even during the rainier periods.

The first thing I did that next morning, as soon as I had my wits about me, was to search for Allegra's letter. Climbing into the attic, I went thumbing through my books for it, but after a few hours of fruitless hunting threw in the towel. The thing had walked off; sometime in the night, apparently, it had disappeared.

Not that I needed the letter to recall what she'd written:

I've made the decision to leave for Palo Alto, but I'd be lying if I said I was happy about it. You're the only one I've ever loved, Michael. I just know that, if I showed up and told you what I was planning, I wouldn't want to go through with it. That's why I've written this letter. It's easier for me this way. Someday, I hope, we'll see each other again. And maybe then we'll be able to talk things through. Maybe this won't be the end for us... if you're ever able to forgive me for breaking things off this way.

It had taken decades, but the two of us had finally had our little reunion—and under far stranger circumstances than either of us could ever have imagined.

MORE CHILLS FROM VELOX BOOKS

MORE CHILLS FROM VELOX BOOKS

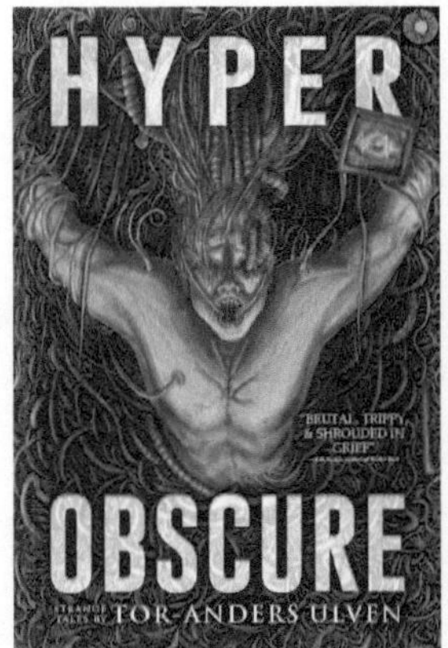

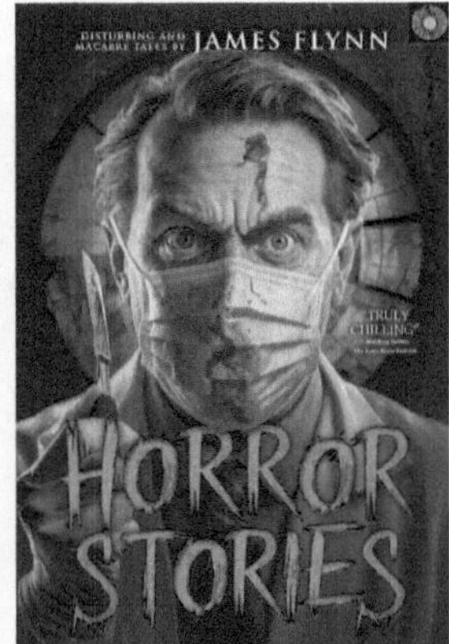